A Very Southern Christmas

A Very Southern Christmas

...

Holiday Stories from the South's Best Writers

...

Edited by
CHARLINE R. MCCORD
and
JUDY H. TUCKER

Preface by
BARRY HANNAH

Illustrated by
WYATT WATERS

ALGONQUIN BOOKS OF CHAPEL HILL 2003

Published by
ALGONQUIN BOOKS OF CHAPEL HILL
Post Office Box 2225
Chapel Hill, North Carolina 27515-2225

a division of
WORKMAN PUBLISHING
708 Broadway
New York, New York 10003

Printed in China.
Published simultaneously in Canada by Thomas Allen & Son Limited.
Design by Anne Winslow.

Library of Congress Cataloging-in-Publication Data
A very southern Christmas : holiday stories from the South's best writers / edited by
    Charline R. McCord and Judy H. Tucker ; preface by Barry Hannah ; illustrated by
    Wyatt Waters.—1st ed.
        p. cm.
    ISBN 1-56512-383-2
    1. Christmas stories, American.   2. Southern States—Social life and customs—
Fiction.   3. Southern States—Social life and customs.   4. American fiction—
Southern States.   5. Christmas—Southern States.   I. McCord, Charline R.
II. Tucker, Judy H.
    PS648.C45C459 2003
    813'.0108334—dc21   2003050246

10   9   8   7   6   5   4   3   2   1
First Edition

Contents

Preface

I HEARD FROM AN OLD movie that you're never really done for if you have a good story and somebody's telling it. You can warm yourself around a good tale. When a tale is really good it becomes the property of the reader as well as the writer. You are lucky here. I know many of these writers and am confident they will not deliver you any but the best work. Into a story goes sacrifice, persistence, and joy. For the holidays, these are just in time. Many folks are depressed around the holidays. These stories are likely to make you feel less lonely.

If I may speak personally, because I've been engaged in longer work lately, I have not written stories in what seems an age now. The result is I am actually ill because of their absence in my life. I would like to have a hand in that marvel that Edgar Allan Poe described so well: the art that should be read at one sitting. The American is rushed (or pretends he is) and he is missing the very thing that is made for him: the short story. Many short pieces have more power and grace than the bulky novel. In fact, the short story offers more freedom, more experimentation than the novel.

The story carries a *light* burden of grace and truth when it is done well. It is said we all write out of nostalgia. Even a mean and brutal story might touch a nostalgic heart and make it glow. Around the holidays, the story bids fair to make us slow down, rest, and find the simplicities. We all know that secular crassness has been in the ascendancy for a long time. Glance at television, the videos. Fast, flashy, vicious, nasty. But please go back and take a study, a happy study of these tales. Back to dogs (even talking animals in good Fred Chappell's story), to authentic people we have disforgotten, and to children, and to babies. And please shed your tears for the absence of Tim McLaurin, the writer who passed from us so recently.

I feel especially sad for Tim's going because we met in the Oxford bookstore just two years ago. We both had about the same disease, but Tim was having a beautiful remission — canoeing, scrambling around happily. He wanted to chat and give me his last book. My God, I had no sense it was to be, truly, his last book. Charline McCord and Judy Tucker give tribute to Tim herein. (I never understood one bit Tim's need for propinquity to great snakes, but God love his weird ways. Thanks also that the writers in this book all stroll down radically separate tracks.)

We do celebrate the infant Christ during this season. Some of us. I do not want to go back there, but I am nostalgic-blue for those animated nativity pageants of my old church when I was a boy. Christ has meant much to me since I dreamed of Him deeply, deeply a week after I nearly died in the hospital. He was dark, stood about six-feet, and had manly wide shoulders, the body of a working man. I do not put this occurrence up to swagger or even convince, believe me. I had never dreamed of Christ, although some of my work seems to have, well, courted him. I *would* like to share with you the absolute peace and simplicity that attended me after that dream-vision, although I was in a world of trouble. I was still nearly dead, and my medical bills in the forthcoming years would be a small fortune. Please, I do not want to direct these excellent writers into Christian service. But many work for a sweet strong Lord who do not realize it. Many serve the Higher Power without will. You can sense extraordinary grace in certain stories that seems to have come without the writer's efforts, even outside his or her provenance.

I celebrate the infant and grown Christ, but even so this world takes over, the stupid and unavailing worries take over. I smoke cigarettes, for godsake. I am a befouled Christian. Almost everybody leads a better life than I do, it seems, with my gaggle of uncontrollable dogs, my vain typewriter. Sometimes I miss the hospital and waking up weeping from that dream in the hospital. The point here is that the world, getting and spending, takes over. But I swear this is true: When I'm telling a good story to my students here at Ole Miss, if I'm good, sweetness and light take over. The same as when they write their good stories for me. No puny magic land here. This is direct soul, brothers and sisters.

This is what I bring you to: the story that moves you deeply and then discreetly off the page in its brevity. It gives you the happiness and heft you will find in few other places. This is not an era for the story, it might seem. Even the male-spun long dirty joke is rare. People are not apt to listen to over five words at a time. You know it; I know it. I challenge you to be rare. Have the quiet moments, the tranced concentration, the sometimes near-sacred illuminations of the beginning, middle, and end, as in a small cathedral.

I'm envious. By God, I wish I were in this collection. I want to speak of peace and simplicity and the small acts of kindness that make the major part of my world. The writers here will speak of these matters, however, along with the harsh muddles that belong equally to the tale teller of any truth. The holiday story that is not merely an occasional piece must embrace the world as we know it. There will be strange, mean, and bewildering Christmases here. Many of us know them personally. One Christmas, with another family, I was so drunk I gave a plant that was already in the room as a Christmas gift to my stepson. To the other stepson I gave my own pocketknife. I was vile and had forgotten Christmas entirely.

I believe the reader may be surprised by the unselfish grace the writer himself feels when a story goes well. I have mentioned my vain typewriter but it is not vain when certain moments come on. These moments are quick, the writing is quick in this writer's case. Lee Smith has mentioned the work she hates as a writer, but surely she does love the work, some of which has traveled by magic, and barely even her own. I write by hand and my best stories are in illegible sprawling ink. Real slop, not even with the dignity of looking foreign. The typing is excruciating. My friendly reader, let me remind you that a writer's life is either strange, compulsive, or fully sick unless it is going on. For example, the sickness I have now for being estranged from the short tale. Many of us stay sick and distracted until we tell these tales, believe me.

As in France, most of us are baptized agnostics. But I believe we are hungry for the substance of faith. We are *wanting* ghosts, such as those who visited Scrooge, to convert us into a simpler, more loving and giving being. We need to see a world where strength brings peace. Most American fiction nowadays simply brings a hunk of something. Very little lifts you to wisdom, and most of it simply belongs to the heralded Information Age. Must we die before we see the open door into bright and sweet heaven? (I've just watched *War and Peace,* in which Prince Andrei—Mel Ferrer— dies with this vision.) *Can* our secular fictions give any deliverance, anyway?

Yes, and especially during these holidays. The writer knows not what he or she writes. Most people who age, I have noticed, become kinder and gentler (in some cases, of course, just lost). The writers will age, will keep the fire, and something will come to them one day that is so simple, so strong, so present, it might look very much like the Christ child Himself.

—Barry Hannah

Introduction

MANY GOOD AND SURPRISING things come from volunteering our time. We met while working as volunteers at the 1996 Eudora Welty Festival in Jackson, Mississippi. We became friends and then members of the same writing group. In 1999, we began collaborating on a collection of stories by Mississippi writers that was published in 2001 as *Christmas Stories from Mississippi* (University Press of Mississippi). The book was beautifully illustrated by Mississippi artist Wyatt Waters, and it quickly took on a life of its own and literally became a Christmas miracle.

It is our belief that good writing is always a miracle — a year-round, ongoing miracle that extends itself by giving to all times, all places, all people. The ten writers represented here are among the South's most outstanding contemporary truth tellers. Some of them confront us with hard truths — truths that demonstrate that human nature is the same yesterday and today, and, undoubtedly, that it will be the same tomorrow. A writer is, among other things, a keen observer of human nature, and those who appear in this collection are some of our keenest and best observers. Through their writings, they hold up a mirror and allow us to pause and reflect on the human condition, and what better time to take inventory than at the close of a year, at Christmastime?

Christmas . . . that enchanted day we all march toward with such incredibly high expectations, *magical* expectations! Surely we are bound to wind up a little disappointed when the magic fails to materialize, when the day arrives feeling very much like any other day. The writers of the stories that follow have all reflected on this most important day of the year, and their observations do not disappoint. Here they capture those magical expectations and deliver them to us in the richness and longevity of the printed word. In their telling of these various tales, they expose our ever-present humanness and our enduring connection to all other humans.

And it is in the spirit of that connectedness that we dedicate this collection to the memory of North Carolina writer Tim McLaurin, who died on July 11, 2002, of complications from esophageal cancer. Tim was only forty-eight years old. He was working on a story idea for our book at the time of his death; we talked several times by phone about it. He never mentioned his illness, not once, only that he *would* write us a story. When the story didn't arrive by our deadline, we learned from editor Kathy Pories at Algonquin that Tim had died. It was a crushing and difficult truth to absorb. Good, brave, larger-than-life Tim McLaurin. Tim . . . such a slight name for such an enormous presence . . . and now an equally enormous absence. Tim the snake handler, Tim the marine, Tim the Peace Corps volunteer in Africa, Tim the father, Tim the husband of a mere two years, Tim the college professor . . . Tim the

Southern writer. We not only wanted Tim in this anthology, we longed for the miracle of his voice again. We contacted Carol, Tim's wife, and together we combed his work for a Christmas selection. We settled on an excerpt from his memoir *Keeper of the Moon*, a Christmas essay we've titled "This Charmed Day," which opens this collection. Within the text of this family story, Tim delivers a line that rings so true that the reader has an immediate "zero at the bone" reaction—the reaction Emily Dickinson relates in her poem "A Narrow Fellow in the Grass"—and a reaction that Tim no doubt encountered often in his advocacy for narrow fellows. As you read the following stories, it is our hope that you will remember a good man and a fine writer, Tim McLaurin, a Southern boy who loved life, loved family, loved stories . . . and that you will ponder that sobering yet truthful line of his, that "joy goes fist in hand with heartbreak"—yes, even at Christmas, perhaps especially at Christmas.

—*Charline R. McCord and Judy H. Tucker*

A Very Southern Christmas

This Charmed Day

by Tim McLaurin

A goose to my rear end, and I might have decapitated myself and risen headless there in the early morning hours of Christmas. I was on my hands and knees, thrust through the broken pane of a French door that divided the living room from the kitchen. Beyond that door lay our Christmas toys set in separate piles, the wrapping paper catching the light from the tree and glinting like a small, unique galaxy. I was peeping at our coveted toys without waking my mother, who slept lightly in the next room.

"What you see?" Bruce whispered loudly, nudging me with his foot. "Let me look."

What I saw was a wonderful scene of packages wrapped quickly in Christmas paper, a fir tree cut from the woods behind our house and dressed in tinsel, glass balls, strings of holly berries, and popcorn, a sock from each of our feet nailed to the mantel and stuffed with fruit and candy. The air smelled of greenery and citrus fruit. I withdrew my head reluctantly, tucking in my chin to clear the edge of the broken pane.

My brothers and sister and I all went insane each year in late

November. The first holiday catalog, usually either from Kmart or Sears or JCPenney, infected us. We'd rip through the pages, eyes bugging at the collection of trucks, bikes, games, cap pistols, and other cheap toys. Within the first week we wanted a hundred different things but then would have to narrow the list to fit the number of gifts my mother decided we could budget. The number usually ran around five presents of our choice, plus a surprise. Our Christmas gifts were supposed to supply our year except for something on our birthday, maybe a toy boat or airplane purchased in midsummer. Each selection was made with careful thought and agony, hours spent poring over slick pages. Our choices reflected much of our individual ages and personalities.

My sister, Karen, two years my senior, was the firstborn. She inherited my mother's brown eyes and hair and gentle, nurturing character. Her choices for Christmas were the same as most other girls', baby dolls and tea sets when little, later on LPs of the Beatles and Tommy James and the Shondells, clothes and dime-store makeup as she grew into adolescent and teenage years. As a female and big sister to four younger brothers, she suffered most in the hard financial years of our youth. She was acutely aware of the appearance of our house, the lack of an indoor toilet, her often outdated fashion in clothes. I remember her tears of frustration and shame when my brothers and I would burst laughing from behind a tree or fence where we had spied on her attempts to learn the steps to the Twist or Mashed Potato. She endured, usually behind a forced smile. When I was thirteen, and my parents built the small brick house that stands as the homeplace today, she was rewarded with her own room, while the brothers continued to sleep two to a bed. Today, she has been married for twenty years, her warm eyes and smile untainted. Her oldest son will soon graduate from the state university, the vanguard of what I hope is a new tradition for his brothers and cousins.

Bruce was born eighteen months following me. He has always been a meat-and-potato man, quiet in his thoughts and quick to anger. When eating dinner, he devours each item on his plate in turn before changing to another food. As a child, his toys were things with wheels—trucks as a kid, a bicycle when his legs were long enough. Today, he drives a semi for Yellow Freight, will give you the shirt off his back if he thinks you need it, but is still as guarded in revealing feelings and thoughts as the tousle-haired child I slept with.

Keith, the knee baby of our family, as child and man is a curious mixture of Bruce and myself. As a kid, he also loved toy trucks and dirt, but was also the only one of my siblings who shared my interest in looking through my telescope. As a kid, he was a bit of a crybaby, a tendency that Bruce exaggerated almost daily for having bumped him from Mama's knee. Once when we were kids and piling brush my father had cut to clear a pasture, he announced with wide eyes and extreme seriousness, "We are really here on earth. We are really alive."

"Of course we're really alive, dummy," the rest of us hooted and laughed.

"But have you ever thought about it?" he continued above our catcalls. "We're really alive."

As a teenager he experimented heavily with drugs and rebelled most against my parents. The philosopher in him thrives today. He repairs heating and air-conditioning units now, owns a Harley, but is happily married and the father of two children. I talk most easily with him of life and the possible afterlife; he likes to sit in the cool of the evening and watch his nesting martins swoop in while he daydreams of riding his bike slowly across America. I doubt he ever will. He realizes his fantasy of traveling *Easy Rider*–style across the country would suffer at the reality of busy highways, hot, dry air, and bugs in his teeth.

Danny is the last of the brothers, born a year following Keith. He was a skinny, silent child, so timid he had to repeat the first grade. We'd trade him nickels for dimes by comparing the size or persuade him to do our chores with simple words of praise. For Christmas, he loved anything that was wrapped and new, but could spend hours playing with a shoe box dragged on a string. Today, all that has changed. He grew into a six-foot-three-inch electric company linesman with arms the size of my calves. He is gregarious, lives at home with my mother, loves the land, animals, and open spaces.

I never believed in Santa or the Easter Bunny or the Tooth Fairy. Even at age eight, the thought of a man who flew in a sleigh pulled by reindeer didn't hold water for me—a kid who had seen Saturn through his telescope. None of us kids believed in Santa, but that did nothing to dampen our enthusiasm. We knew our gifts were bought during our mother's Tuesday trips to town and hidden at Mrs. Bell's house. She was our closest neighbor, a quarter mile down the road. Tuesday was payday for my father, and Mama would drive into town to get his check, cash it, buy groceries, and pay past-due bills. We would sneak across the field when we saw Mama pass our house on her return, and watch through the bushes as she made a couple of trips into the old woman's home, carrying oddly shaped paper sacks.

The days till Christmas crept past agonizingly slow. Two weeks before Christmas, school let out for the holiday. I began marking the days off on a calendar. This was still in the days when television holiday specials and cartoons were pretty scarce except for maybe a Bing Crosby White Christmas Special. The Grinch and Charlie Brown and all those characters were still on comic pages or in people's minds. Chores were scarce in the winter, and with no homework there was not much to do all day but hunch over the catalogs and mentally play with our new toys. We scanned the sky and hoped for signs of snow, but I can remember maybe one real snowy Christmas in my life. With a few days to spare, my father found a shapely fir in the forest and cut it and brought it home. My mother kept a large box of tree decorations in a closet top, and the first night of the tree we trimmed her with glass globes and fake ice tinsel and those fat, nonblinking colored lights. We strung red holly berries and popcorn on sewing thread. The presents my mother bought for her brother and for my grandparents were wrapped and placed under the tree. Karen gathered us boys in the bedroom and reminded us that we'd bought nothing for our own parents. We planned a secret trip to the store. We had only a few quarters between us, maybe a wrinkled dollar, some dimes and nickels. The money was found in either the washing machine or by searching the folds of the couch and armchair. I explained to Mama that we needed another dollar, but I couldn't tell her why we needed the money or why we all needed to walk to Mrs. Smith's store. She nodded and faked ignorance.

Walking through Beard, we gawked at the Christmas trees and wreaths decorating our neighbors' houses. We bought my father a jar of Aqua Velva shaving lotion, my mother a pair of hose and a box of chocolate-covered cherries. Somehow, the money Karen held in her fist was just enough to satisfy Mrs. Smith. She nodded and smiled over our good choices, even added a few pieces of penny candy to the sack. We slipped the presents into the house and wrapped them with newspaper and baling twine.

Christmas Eve finally arrived. That day has always held a magical quality for me. The air is clear and sweet. Even cold rain beads on tree limbs and wilted grass like jewels. We always gave the animals a little extra feed, a pat on the head or scratch on the belly for the tame pig or cow. I had read that animals talked on Christmas Eve, and though I didn't believe it, I liked to imagine they would speak highly of us for the extra rations. The day dragged by impossibly slow; we scanned the catalogs again and worried that we had not chosen the right toys. We printed our names on school paper with big letters in crayon and taped the cards to spots in the living room where we wanted our gifts stacked. I read to my brothers stories about the red-nosed reindeer, the baby Jesus, and Santa. We dressed and prepared for bed early, even though usually we were as hard to get in bed as we were to get up in the morning. The house had no central heat; I remember glasses filled with water and left by our beds crusted with ice occasionally on very cold nights. Mama warmed our pillows on top of the living room heater, and when they were close to scorching, we dived under the cold covers, private heaters in hand. As always at night, she read us a passage from the Bible, then prayed. Of course, on this night she read us again the story of when the angels visited the Christ child. Her last words were for us not to budge from bed until she called us the next morning.

Soon after the lights were out in our room, I heard the truck crank up in the yard. My brothers and I scurried from our twin beds, Karen from her cot that sat in the corner of the same bedroom. We all gathered at the window and watched the taillights as my parents drove up to Mrs. Bell's to fetch our gifts. After a few minutes, they returned, and we heard their whispers as they brought armloads of presents into the living room. Occasionally we heard them laugh, the clunk of heavy objects, the clink of tools needed to put something together. The air smelled of coffee mixed with the good odor of pine boughs and orange peel. Finally, the noise stopped, and I knew my mother and father were retiring for a few hours before he had to rise and go to work at the bakery. My brothers were sleeping, air whistling through their mouths. I tied my alarm to one of my big toes.

My alarm was made of several tin cans tied close on a string so they could rattle. The string was looped through a nail driven into the ceiling and bent double, then tied securely to my toe. My theory was that when I slept I always pulled my knees close to my belly. If I went to sleep on Christmas Eve—perish the thought— I'd wake myself when I drew my legs up by rattling the cans. String tied in place, I lay stiff on my back, legs stretched straight, and imagined what all those gifts would look like stacked under the colored lights.

I always went to sleep, the alarm never quite worked, but always somehow I awakened in the early morning hours, usually a couple of hours before sunrise. I bolted up in bed, jerked the string from my toe, then sneaked to the closed door and listened to hear that all was quiet. Then I woke up everyone and we trooped to the French doors.

My father always worked on Christmas Day, usually reporting to work about four in the morning. I never remember him watching us open the gifts that he worked such long hours to provide. In his youth, he had been one of seven children raised during the Depression. If the fall crops had produced well, he might get a fresh orange for Christmas, or if he was very lucky, an article of clothing. I thought that impossibly sad. My mother had grown up easier. Her mother was a nurse, her father a clerk. But their failed marriage caused her to spend many of her holidays rotating between two households. Though my father could not express his feelings in words, I know that as he cranked his old truck and drove away from our lighted windows on those early Christmas mornings he left in pride. Through the window were warm sleeping children, a wife he loved, wholesome food, and a tree surrounded with gifts.

Our whispered chatter woke up my mother. She warned us to get back in bed. We obeyed her for a few minutes, then lined up to peek again. About six in the morning, the sun still an hour and a half from rising, we begged her from bed. She made us lie down again while she turned up the kerosene fire to warm the living room. Finally, she told us to line up, opened the French door, and said, "Go!"

I hold mild contempt for people who have the restraint to open gifts by carefully removing the ribbon and unsticking the tape. We flew into our gifts, elbows and hands a blur, shredding paper and tearing through pasteboard and plastic. The first gift was pulled from the box, given about two seconds attention, and laid aside, another started on. After the last gift was opened, the socks were pulled from the nails on the shelf, contents spilled on the floor— fruit and hard candy, maybe a plastic racing car. We sat with our gifts stacked between our legs, our mouths filled with candy, and looked and touched and gaped for a few moments before sorting out which one to begin playing with first.

The scientist in me showed through at Christmas. My choices from the catalogs were plastic dinosaurs, a chemistry set, a battleship, and a launchable rocket. As the room warmed, play began, a race of toy trucks around the couch, under bombardment from my scale destroyer, G.I. Joe attacked by a brontosaurus. The play rocked the cluttered room while we waited for the sun to rise enough to allow us outside, and the air filled with the good smell of eggs cooking along with bacon.

Joy goes fist in hand with heartbreak. I can't remember a Christmas that a bicycle was not pulled from the crate minus the handlebars, a toy truck with a broken wheel.

When I shot a spring-loaded missile from my battleship toward Keith's truck, the missile arced across the room and landed on top of the kerosene heater, slipped between the slats on the grille, and fell on top of the scalding fire drum. Despite my frantic attempts to retrieve the missile, before my eyes it shriveled, then caught fire and burned, filling the room with black smoke and a terrible smell.

On another Christmas, dawn finally illuminated the fields and pasture. The day was blustery; a chill north wind blew that was mixed with sleet. I carried my rocket outside. The foot-long missile launched on a thick rubber band was supposed to dart skyward a couple hundred feet, then return to earth by parachute. I stood in the front yard and slung that rocket into the air, saw it leap toward the clouds, where it hung for a moment, then began to fall. The top of the rocket opened, the chute unfurled and blossomed. The launch was perfect. I jumped up and down shouting with joy and excitement until I realized how strong the wind was. The last I saw of the rocket, it was whipping back and forth on the breeze as it traveled over the tops of several distant trees.

But there were other presents inside. The loss of one rocket, a truck minus a wheel, or a baby doll minus her bottle, could never spoil such a day.

We ate Christmas dinner at midday at my Granddaddy Raymond's house. He was my mother's dad, a big man with a quick temper who never was very fond of small children. He was married the second time to a woman named Mollie who was very sure she didn't like step-grandchildren. We sat on the couch like timid mice and waited for dinner. Mollie brewed tea without sugar, the bitter drink sharply contrasting with the sugary concoction my mother made. In trying to drink Mollie's tea, I gained one of my first realizations that the world had no set rules.

My granddaddy gave us socks for Christmas. All of us, even Danny when he was barely out of diapers, got socks. That was also one of my earliest lessons in learning that sometimes it was important and polite to lie.

"Oh boy! Look, Mama, I got socks," I said, holding up my pair.

"I did too," Karen said.

"Me too," my brothers sadly echoed. We waved our socks like flags.

We usually ate supper at Granny's house. She was Mama's mother, a very serious woman who didn't even give us socks for Christmas. She did have something that more than compensated. She had a color television. She picked us up in her car in the midafternoon and drove us to her house, where we watched the Christmas specials, sitting close to the screen as if we were glued there.

My father met us after work at Granny's. He arrived in his white uniform, the creases dusted with flour, his person smelling of freshly baked bread. We gave him the gift we had bought with his money, and for a few moments he let down his guard, smiled, and even joked. He shook the gift, weighed it in his hand, smelled it, and listened to it for a clue. He guessed wrong. After tearing off the paper and faking surprise he opened the bottle and smelled it and smiled.

"Your eyes may shine, your teeth may grit," he said, "but this here present you ain't gonna get."

We howled with delight. He set the bottle back down, probably never to touch it again. We glued ourselves to the next color television program while baking mincemeat and sweet potato pie filled the house with good smells. As the day fell into shadow, I realized sadly that another Christmas was rapidly passing, and that the wonderful anticipation and enchantment of awaiting Christmas Day was worth much more than a lapful of opened presents. Christmas rose high above reality, was a time when a child or parent could truly believe in Santa Claus, the Christ child, and reindeer that flew. Maybe the new year would bring a bout of flu, disease might strike the hogs, and the bills would start to roll in. But for a brief few weeks those worries seemed trivial when compared to one's dreams. My father as a boy had delighted in a fresh orange for Christmas; he and my mother gave me plastic rocket ships. But more important, in the warm glow of that kerosene heater, I possessed the security and confidence that one day I might fly a real rocket to the moon. I could give no more valuable gift to my own children today than that trust. Tear into that tinsel, child, through ribbon and cardboard, cast it all aside, and go for what you know lies inside. Worry about the future next week or the next; this charmed day, this era in your life, will pass too soon.

Deputy Sid's Gift

by Tim Gautreaux

I'm going to tell you about the last time I went to confession. I met this priest at the nursing home where I work spoon-feeding the parish's old folks. He noticed I had a finger off, and so he knew I was oil field and wanted to know why I was working indoors. This priest was a blond guy with eyes you could see through and didn't look like nobody inside of two hundred miles of Grand Crapaud, Louisiana. He didn't know that when sweet crude slid under twelve dollars a barrel, most oil companies went belly-up like a stinking redfish, and guys like me had to move out or do something else. So I told him I took a night class in scrubbing these old babies, and he said I had a good heart and bull like that and invited me to come visit at the rectory if I ever needed to.

One day I needed to, yeah. Everybody's got something they got to talk about sometime in their life. I went to the old brick church on LeBlanc Street on a Saturday morning and found him by himself in his little kitchen in the old cypress priest house, and we sat down by the table with a big pot of coffee.

So I told him what had been going through my head, how I

used to have a 1962 Chevrolet pickup truck, a rusty spare I kept parked out by the road just to haul off trash. It was ratty and I was ashamed to drive it unless I was going to the dump. One day after Christmas my wife, Monette, told me to get rid of the tree and the holiday junk, so I went to crank the truck. Well, in a minute I'm standing by the road with a key in my hand, looking at a long patch of pale weeds where the truck used to be. I'm saying to myself that the truck coulda been gone a hour or a week. It's just a thing you don't look at unless you need it.

So I called Claude down at his little four-by-four city jail and he said he'd look for it the next day, that he had more expensive stuff to worry about. Ain't that a hell of a note. Then I called the sheriff's office down at the parish seat, and when I told them the truck's over thirty years old, they acted like I'm asking them to look for a stole newspaper or something. It was my truck and I wanted it back.

The priest, he just nodded along and poured us our first cup of coffee from a big aluminum dripolator. When he finished, he put the pot in a shallow pan of water on the gas stove behind his chair and stared down at his shoe, like he was hearing my confession, which I guess he was. He even had his little purple confession rag hanging on his neck.

I told the priest how the cops searched a lil' bit, and how I looked, but that old truck just disappeared like rain on a hot street. Monette, she was glad to get it out the yard, but I needed something for hauling, you know? So after not too long I found a good old '78 Ford for a thousand dollars and bought that and put it right where the other one was.

One day my little girl Lizette and me, we was at the nursing home together because of some student-visit-the-parent-at-work deal at her school. She was letting the old folks hug her little shoulders and pat her dark hair. You know how they are. They see a child and go nuts to get at them, like the youngness is going to wear off on their old bodies. At the end of my shift, one of the visitors who was there to see his dried-up wife—I think he was a Canulette, kind of a café au lait dude from out by Prairie Amère—his truck won't crank, so me and Lizette decided to bring him home. Me in my smocky little fruit uniform and Lizette with her checkerboard school suit went off in my shiny thirdhand Buick, old man Canulette sitting between us like a fence post. We rolled down the highway and turned off into the rice fields and went way back into the tree line toward Coconut Bayou. We passing through that poor folks' section on the other side of Tonga Bend when Lizette stuck her head out the window to make her pigtails go straight in the wind. Next thing I knew, she yelled, Daddy, there's your truck, back in the woods. I turned the car around in that little gravel road and sure enough—you couldn't hardly see it unless you had young eyes—there was my old Chevy parked up under a grove of live oaks maybe 150 yards away.

We walked up on it, and judging from the thistles that had growed up past the bumper, it'd been there three months. I held back and asked Monsieur Canulette if anybody lived around there, and he looked at the truck and said the first word since town: Bezue. He said here and there in the woods a Bezue lived and they all had something wrong in they heads. I told him I'd put me a Bezue in jail if he stole my truck, but he just looked at me with those silver eyes of his in a way that gave me *les frissons*. I brought the old man to his little farm and then came back to Tonga Bend Store to call the deputy, who took most of a hour to get out there.

They sent Sid Touchard, that black devil, and he showed up with his shaggy curls full of pomade falling down his collar, the tape deck in his cruiser playing zydeco. He got out with a clipboard, like he knows how to write, and put on his cowboy hat. He asked me if I was the Bobby Simoneaux what called, and even Lizette looked behind her in the woods for maybe another Bobby Simoneaux, but I just nodded. He looked at the truck and the leaves and branches on it and asked me do I still want it. *Mais*, yeah, I told him. Then Sid walked up and put his hand on the door handle like it was something dirty, which I guess it was, and pulled. What we saw was a lot of trash paper, blankets, and old clothes. I looked close and Lizette stepped back and put her little hands on her mouth. The air was nothing but mildew and armpit, and by the steering wheel was a nappy old head.

He's living in it, Deputy Sid said. His eyebrows went up when he said that. Even he was surprised, and he works the poor folks of the parish. He asked again do I still want it. Hell yeah, I said. He spit. He's a tall man, yeah, and it takes a long time for his spit to hit the ground. Then he reached in and woke the man, who sat up and stared at us. He was black—back-in-the-country black. He wasn't no old man, but he had these deep wrinkles the old folks call the sorrow grooves, and he looked like he was made out of Naugahyde. His eyeballs was black olives floating in hot sauce, and when Sid tried to get out of him what he was doing in the truck, he took a deep breath and looked over the rusty hood toward the road.

Finally he said, I'm Fernest. Fernest Bezue. My mamma, she lives down that way. He pointed, and I could see he been drunk maybe six years in a row. The old cotton jacket he had on was eat up with battery acid and his feet was bare knobs. Sid give me that look like he got on bifocals, but he ain't. Hell no, I told him. I want my truck. He stole it and you got to put him in jail. So Sid said to him, you stole this truck? And Fernest kept looking at the road like it was something he wasn't allowed to see, and then he said he found it here. When he said that, I got hot.

Deputy Sid tugged Fernest out into the sunlight, slow, like he was a old cow he was pulling out a tangle of fence. He put him in the cruiser and told me and Lizette to get in the front seat. He said where Fernest's mamma lived, my Buick can't go. So we rolled down the gravel a mile, turned off on a shell road where the chinaball and sticker bushes about dragged the paint off that beat-up cruiser. Lizette, she sat on my lap, looking at Deputy Sid's candy bar wrappers on the floor, a satsuma on the seat, and a rosary around the rearview. The road gave out at a pile of catbrier and we turned left into a hard-bottom coulee full of rainwater next to Coconut Bayou. The water come up to the hubcaps and

Lizette wiggled and told Deputy Sid we on a ferryboat for sure, yeah.

There's this little shotgun shack up on brick piers with the tar paper rotting off it, stovepipe stub sticking out the side wall, no steps to the door, cypress knees coming up in the yard, egg cartons and water jugs floating around on the breeze. Deputy Sid leaned on the horn for maybe fifteen seconds until the front door opened and a woman look like a licorice stick stood there dressed in some old limp dress. He rolled down the window and asked if it's her son in the backseat. She stooped slow, squinted a long time. That Fernest, she said to the water. She sure wasn't talking to us. Sid stepped out on a walk board and told me to follow. I jacked up my legs, slid over all the junk, and brought out that satsuma with me. Can't leave this with Lizette, I told him. She loves these things. Sid took it from me, tossed it to her, and she caught that with one hand.

While he talked to the woman I looked in the house. All this while, my shoes was filling up with water. The first room had nothing but a mattress and a kerosene lamp on the floor and some bowls next to it. The walls was covered with newspaper to keep the wind out. In the second and last room, the floor had fell in. The whole place was swayback because the termites had eat out the joists and side beams. It didn't take no genius to tell that the roof rafters wasn't gonna last another year. A wild animal would take to a hole in the ground before he lived in a place like that.

Deputy Sid asked the woman did she know about the truck, and she said he was living in it. He turned to me and said, look around. You want me to put him in jail?

Hell yeah, I told him, and Sid looked at me hard with those oxblood eyes he got, trying to figure a road into my head. He told me if I file charges and put him in jail, that'd cost the parish. My tax money was gonna pay to feed him and put clothes on him. He said let him stay with his mamma. The old woman stooped down again, and Fernest stared at her like maybe she was a tractor or a cloud. I looked around again and saw that putting him in jail would be a promotion in life, yeah.

Sid took off the bracelets and walked him to the house. The old lady said he could stay. Then we left, that cruiser bottoming out and fishtailing from the yard, its mud grips digging down to the claypan. Back at my truck I threw all his stuff in a pile, old coats with cigarette holes burnt through, medicine bottles from the free clinic in town, dirty drawers I handled with a stick, fried chicken skin and bones, a little radio with leaking batteries. I put my key in but the engine didn't make a sound. When I opened up the hood, all I saw was a pile of a thousand sticks and three long otter-looking animals that took off for the woods. The sheriff's tow truck brought the thing back to my house and that was that. My wife took one look at it and one smell of it and told me it had to be gone. I already had one truck.

A rainy spell set in and the truck sank down in the backyard for a couple weeks with the crawfish chimneys coming up around it till I got a nice day and scrubbed it inside and out. Down at the home we got five new poor helpless folks from the government without nobody dying to make room for 'em, so another week passed before I could get to the hardware and buy me a nice orange FOR SALE sign.

Now THIS WAS WHEN the priest kind of leaned back against the window frame and made a faraway smile and looked out to the rose garden Father Scheuter put in before they transferred him to Nevada. Priests try not to look you in the eye when you telling stuff. Scared maybe you won't tell it straight, or tell it all. So I told him straight that the second night that old truck was parked back out on the street wearing that sign, it got stole. I called up Deputy Sid direct this time and told him what happened. He said, you want me to look for that truck again? I told him hell yeah. He said, don't you got a truck already? I think that pomade Sid been smearing on his head all these years done soaked in his brain, and I told him that. He said, you got a nice brick house, a wife, three kids, and two cars. He said, you might quit at that. He said he didn't feel like burning fifty dollars gas looking for a forty-dollar truck. I told him I would talk to the sheriff, and he said okay, he'd look.

I wound up at the home helping out for music day, when Mr. Lodrigue brings his Silvertone guitar and amp to play songs the old folks recognize. Man, they love that rusty stuff like "As Time Goes By," "The Shrimp Boats Is A-Coming," and such 78 rpm tunes they can tap their feet to. I get a kick out of them people— one foot in the grave and still trying to boogie. And Mr. Lodrigue, who has wavery silver hair and kind of smoky gray eyes, he looks like Frank Sinatra to them old gals.

I got through with music day and went out to where my car was at behind the home, and there, big as a hoss, was Sid sitting on the hood of his muddy police car. I walked up and saw his arms was crossed. He said, I found it. I asked him where it was, and he said, where it was before. I said, you mean Fernest Bezue got it back in Prairie Amère? Man, that made me hot. Here I let him go free and he comes back on me like that. I cursed and spit twice. Deputy Sid looked at me like I was the thief. I asked him why didn't he haul him in, and he looked away. Finally, he said, he's alcoholic. That got me hotter. Like *I* could go down to Generous Gaudet's used-car lot drunk and steal me a car and somebody would let *me* off. Deputy Sid nodded, but he said, Simoneaux, you play with those old people like they your own *grandpère* and *grandmère*. You don't know what they done wrong in they time. I sat down next to him when he said that. The hood metal popped in and shook loose a thought in my head that kind of got me worried. It was about the folks in the home. Maybe I was nice to the old people because I was paid for that. Nobody was paying me to be nice to a drunk Bezue from Prairie Amère. I spit on the sidewalk and wondered if Deputy Sid's as dumb as he looks. Then I thought about Fernest Bezue out under the oaks, staring at the road. So I said, okay, get the tow truck to pull it in, and he says, no, I can't make a report because they'll pick him up.

What you think about that? I got to go get my own stole truck, yeah. That's my tax dollars at work.

THE POT ON THE RANGE gave a little jump like a steam bubble got caught under its bottom, and the priest turned and got us another cup. He was frowning a little now, like his behind's hurting in that hard-bottom chair, but he didn't say anything, still didn't look.

I went on about how I wanted to do the right thing, how me and Monette got out on the gravel past Prairie Amère, trying to beat a big thunderstorm coming up from the Gulf. When we got to where the truck was, the wind was twisting those live oaks like they was rubber. Monette stayed in the Buick and I walked up to the old red truck, and in the bed was Fernest, sitting down with a gallon of T&T port between his legs, just enjoying the breeze. You stole my truck again, I told him. He said he had to have a place to get away. He said it like he was living in a vacation home down on Holly Beach. He was staring up into the black cloud bank, waiting for lightning. That's how people like him live, I guess, waiting to get knocked down and wondering why it happens to them. I looked at his round head and that dusty nap he had for hair and started to walk off. But he had what was mine and he didn't work for it, and I figured it would do him more harm than good to just give him something for nothing. I said if he could get two hundred dollars he could have the truck. I didn't know where that come from, but I said it. He said if he had two hundred dollars he wouldn't be sitting in the woods with a five-dollar gallon of wine. I wondered for a minute where he wanted to go, but just for a minute, because I didn't want to get in his head. So I looked in the cab where he'd hot-wired the ignition, and I sparked up that engine. I pulled out his blankets and some paper bags of food and threw them in a pile. Then I jumped into the bed and put down the tailgate. I had to handle him like the real helpless ones at the home, he was that drunk, and even in that wind he smelled sour, like a wet towel bunched up in the trunk. I put the truck in gear and left him in the middle of that clearing under them oaks, him that wouldn't pay or work. When I rolled up on the road ahead of Monette in the Buick, the rain come like a water main broke in the sky. I looked back at Fernest Bezue and he was standing next to his pile of stuff, one finger in that jug by his leg and his head up like he was taking a shower. Then a big bolt come down across the road and the rain blew sideways like busted glass, and I headed back for town.

All that night I rolled like a log in the bed. I thought the weather would blow over, but the storm set on Grand Crapaud like a flat iron and dropped big welding rods of lightning almost till dawn. On the way to work I got tempted to drive back to Prairie Amère, but I didn't, and all that day I was forgetting to change bed linen and was slopping food on the old babies when I fed 'em. It took me a week to relax, to get so I could clean the truck some more without seeing Fernest looking up at the sky, waiting. I got it ready and put it on the lawn, but this time I took the battery and left it in the carport. Nobody looked at it for about a week. One morning Lizette, she kissed me bye and went out to wait for the bus. A minute later I heard the screen door open and Lizette said the old truck was trying to run. She said it was making running noise. So I went out and looked through the glass. Fernest Bezue was in there snoring on his back like a sawmill. When Lizette found out it was a big drunk man she yelled and ran for the house. She was scared, yeah, and I didn't like that. I opened the driver door and it took me five minutes to convince him I wasn't Mr. Prudhomme, a cane farmer he used to work for ten years back. When he sat up, his left eye capsized, then come back slow, and it was weak, like a lamp flame at sunup. He stared out the windshield at a place I couldn't see.

I told Fernest that I ought to pull him out and turn the hose on him for scaring my little girl like he did. He mumbled something I didn't catch, and I told him to get the hell away. But he just sat there in the middle of that old sprung bench seat like he half-expected me to get in and drive him somewhere to eat. Finally he told me the house had fell in and his mamma went off somewhere and didn't tell him. Man, I let him have it. Told him to stop that drink and get a job. He said that his drinking was a disease, and I told him yeah, it was a *lazy* disease. He said if he could help it, he would. That his daddy was the same way and died in a wreck. I told him he was in a slow wreck right now. I looked back at my house and them wilting camelias Monette planted under the windows. Then I told him if he could stay dry for a week I'd see if I could get him a mopping job at the rest home. He could save up and buy my truck. Then he put his head down and laughed. I can't stop, man, he said to me. That pissed me off so bad I went in and called the cops. After a while Claude come up in the town's cruiser, took one look at Fernest, then looked over where I'm standing by my Japan plum tree. How they made a gun belt skinny enough for that man, I don't know. He asked me, *mais,* what you 'spec us to do with him? Claude is real country, can't hardly talk American. He said Fernest can't do nothing to that truck he can arrest him for. If he steal it again the mayor gonna give him the town beutimfication award. I said arrest him, and I could see in Claude's eyes that nobody was on the night shift to keep a watch on Fernest down at that one-cell jail. Do something, I told him. He's scaring Lizette sleeping out here.

What Claude did is put him in the squad car, stop by Bug's café and buy him a ham sandwich, and drop him off at the town limits, by the abandoned rice mill buildings. They told me that when I called the station later on.

THIS WAS WHEN the priest got up and stretched. He pointed to my cup and I shook my head. He fixed himself one more with lots of cream, got a glass of water from the tap, and sat down again, looking at me just once, real quick.

That made me feel like I could keep going, so I told him how that night and a couple nights more I couldn't sleep without dreaming something about that no-good drunk. I mean, lots of people need help. My one-legged uncle needs his grass cut, and I'd do it, but he says he don't want me to mess with it. Says I got better things to do with my time. Other people deserve my help, and that

Fernest didn't deserve nothing, yet when I went to sleep, there he was in my head. When I read a newspaper, there he was in a group picture, until I focused real good. But after a while he started to fade again, you know, like before. I settled into business at the home, putting ointment on the bald men's heads, putting Band-Aids on the old ladies' bunions so they can wear shoes, though there's no place for them to walk to.

Then one morning here she come, in with three poor folks the government paid us to take, Fernest's mamma, all dried up like beef jerky. She had herself a stroke out on Mr. Prudhomme's farm, where she was staying for free in a trailer, and one side of her wouldn't work. I stayed away from her for three days, until it was time for Mr. Lodrigue, the music man, when everybody gets together in the big room. I was just walking by to get Mr. Boudreaux his teeth he left in the pocket of his bathrobe when her good arm stuck out and grabbed my fruity little uniform. I didn't want to look in her eye, but I did. She slid out her tongue and wet her lips. The mailbox is the onliest thing standing, she told me. The house fall in. I told her it's a shame and I wanted to walk away, but she got hold of my little smock and balled it in her fist.

She told me his government check come in the mailbox, then he walk five miles for the wine. She told me he was gonna die of the wine and couldn't I help. I looked at her and I felt cold as a lizard. I asked her why me. She said, you the one. I told her he was past all help. He had the drinking disease and that was that. I pulled away and went got old man Boudreaux's choppers, and when I come back I saw her across the room, pointing at me with the one finger what would still point. You the one, that finger said. I laughed and told myself right then and there I wasn't going to help no black drunk truck thief that couldn't be helped.

THE PRIEST, HE MADE to swat a mosquito on his arm, but he changed his mind and blew it away with his breath. I didn't know if he was still listening good. Who knows if a priest pays a lot of attention. I think you supposed to be talking to God, and the man in the collar is just like a telephone operator. Anyway, I kept on.

I told him how after work I used the phone out in the parking lot to call Deputy Sid to help me find Fernest. Yeah, I was ashamed of myself. I didn't know what I was going to do if Sid found him for me, but I had to do something to get the old lady's pointing finger out my head. I went home, and about a hour before sundown Deputy Sid pulled up in my front yard and I went out to him, carrying Lizette, who had a cold and was all leechy like a kid gets when she's feeling bad. Sid had him a long day. His pomade hair hung down like a thirsty azalea. He said we got to go out to Prairie Amère, and so I put my little girl down, got in the old truck, and followed him out.

We went through the pine belt and past the rice fields those Thibodeaux boys own, and by them poor houses in Tonga Bend, then we broke out into Prairie Amère, which is mostly grass and weed flowers with a live oak every now and then, but no crops. The old farmers say everything you plant there comes up with a bitter taste. All of a sudden the cruiser pulled off into the clover on the side of the road, so I rolled up behind. There ain't a thing around, and I walked up and Deputy Sid said empty land is a sad thing. He stretched and I could hear his gun belt creaking. I asked why we stopped and he pointed. Maybe a hundred yards in the field, eat up by weeds, was a little barn, the kind where a dozen cows could get in out the sun. We jumped the ditch and scratched through the buttonbush and bull tongue. Deputy Sid stopped once and sneezed. He said I told him to find Fernest and he did. It wasn't easy, but he did. He asked what did I want with him, and I said his mamma wanted me to check, but that wasn't it, no. It was the people at the home what made me do it. I was being paid to be nice to them. I wanted to do something without being paid. I didn't give a damn about some black truck thief, but I wanted to help him. I couldn't tell Deputy Sid this.

We got to the tin overhang on the barn, and we wasn't able to see much inside. The sun was about down. We stepped in and waited for our eyes to get used to the place. I could smell that peppery-sweet cypress. A building can be a hundred years old— if it's made of cypress, you going to smell that. Along the side wall was a wooden feed rack three feet off the ground, and sleeping in there was Fernest, his face turned to that fine-grain wall. Deputy Sid let out a little noise in his throat like a woman would make. He said Fernest was trying to sleep above the ground so the ants couldn't get to him. He said one time two years before, Fernest passed out on the ground and woke up in blazes with a million fire ants all over him like red pepper in a open wound. He stayed swole up for three weeks with hills of running pus all over him, and when his fever broke, he was half blind and mostly deaf in one ear.

I went over to the feed trough and shook him. He smelled strong and it took five minutes before he opened his eyes, and even in the dark you could see them glowing sick. I asked him was he all right and he asked me if I was his mamma, so I waited a minute for his head to get straight. Deputy Sid came close and picked up a empty bottle and sniffed it. I reached through the slats and bumped Fernest's arm and asked him why he drank so damn much when he knew it would kill him. He looked up at me like I was stupid. He said the booze was like air to him. Like water. I told him maybe I could get him picked up and put in the crazy house, and Sid told me no, he's not crazy, he's just drunk all the time. The state thinks there's a difference. Fernest sat up in the trough, hay all stuck in his hair, and he started coughing deep and wet, like some of the old folks do at the home late in the evening. Night shift is scary because them babies sail away in the dark. Anyway, Fernest's face got all uneven, and he asked me what I wanted. That stopped me. I opened my dumb mouth just to see what would come out, and I told him that Deputy Sid bought my truck and was giving it to him so he could stay in it sometime. I held up the key and gave it to him. He nodded like he expected this, like people wake him up all the time and give him cars. I looked at Sid and I could see a gold star on a tooth, but he stayed quiet. Then I told Fernest I knew he couldn't drive it, and I was going take the insurance off anyway, but he could use it to sleep out of the weather like he done before. He looked at Sid and reached out and gave him some kind of boogaloo handshake. In a minute I had the truck up in the grass by the barn, and I pulled the battery out just in case, and Deputy

Sid brought me and the battery toward home. We pulled away from all that flat, empty land, and after about five miles Sid asked why I told Fernest *he* gave him the car. I looked at a tornado-wrecked trailer on the side the road and said I didn't want nothing for what I did. The cruiser rattled past the poor folks in Tonga Bend, and Sid tuned in a scratchy zydeco station. Clinton Rideau and the Ebony Crawfish started pumping out "Sunshine Can't Ruin My Storm," but I didn't feel like tapping my foot.

I went home and expected to sleep, but I didn't. I thought I did something great, but by two A.M., I knew all I did was give away a trashy truck with the floor pans rusting out and all the window glass cracked. I gave up the truck mostly to make myself feel good, not to help Fernest Bezue. And that's what I told the priest I come there to tell him.

The priest looked at me in the eyes then, and I could see something coming, like a big truck or a train. Then he leaned in and I could smell the soap on him. He told me there's only one thing worse than what I did. I looked at the linoleum and asked, what's that? And he said, not doing it.

I like to fell out the chair.

About a month later Fernest's mamma died in the night, and I called up Deputy Sid at dawn. He went out to look but he couldn't find Fernest nowhere. Sid brought his big black self to my house, and I saw him bouncing up my drive like he got music in his veins instead of blood. He got on a new khaki uniform tight as a drumhead, knife creases all over. He told me the liquor store past Coconut Bayou said they ain't seen him. The mailbox at the old place been eat down by termites. None of the farmers seen him. I said it's a shame we can't tell him about his mamma, and Deputy Sid looked at me sidewise and kissed his lips like he's hiding a smile. I told him to come inside, and Monette fixed us all a cup of coffee, and we sat down in the kitchen and cussed the government.

Summer come and the weather turned hot as the doorknob to hell. The old babies at the home couldn't roll around outside, so we had to keep 'em happy in the big room by playing cards and like that. I had to play canasta with six ladies who couldn't remember the rules between plays, so I would spend three hours a day explaining rules to a game we'd never finish.

I guess it was two months after Fernest's mamma passed. I got home and sat in my easy chair by the air condition when Lizette come by and give me a little kiss and said Deputy Sid wanted me on the phone. So I went in the kitchen, and he told me he's in his cruiser out at Mr. Thibaut's place in the north end of the parish, west of Mamou. He found Fernest.

I couldn't say nothing for half a minute. I asked him was he drunk, and he said no, he was way past that, and I said when, and he said he died about yesterday in the truck. I got a picture of Fernest Bezue driving that wreck on the back roads, squinting through the cracked windshield, picking his spot for the night. I told Deputy Sid I was sorry and he said, don't feel like that. He said, we couldn't do nothing for him but we did it anyway.

New Dresses

by Mary Ward Brown

Mrs. Lovelady, in a morning-fresh white uniform, helped Lisa's mother-in-law, Mrs. Worthy, in the car. Lisa could only stand by and watch. The bucket seat was too low and dangerously tilted for Mrs. Worthy as she was now, and Lisa wished she had listened to David, had come in his car instead of her own as he'd tried to tell her. Mrs. Lovelady kept smiling, for Mrs. Worthy's sake. Her eyes froze over when she looked at Lisa.

Mrs. Worthy had been a Laidlaw of Virginia, and before her illness she had looked it. Good clothes, her grandmother's jewelry, those quadruple-A shoes. Today she had on an old London Fog coat buttoned up to the chin. She was so thin it fell from her shoulders as from a hanger. On her head was a plain dark hat, to hide the loss of hair, Lisa supposed. She wore none of her rings. Only the yellow-gold wedding band she never took off.

Mrs. Lovelady handed in a cane with a wide silver band. "Got your medicine?" she asked.

Mrs. Worthy patted her purse and smiled. Her smile was too bright, like the wrong shade of lipstick.

Off at last, she didn't look back, though Mrs. Lovelady watched and waved from the walk. Behind Mrs. Lovelady was the portico of Mrs. Worthy's house, family home of her late husband. With its tall square columns and porches upstairs and down, the house stood as it had for over a century, through good times and bad, including wars that had cost the family a son in each generation. A driveway, where leaves and acorns crunched beneath the wheels of the car, made a deep half-circle in front.

It was the end of November, and trees on the grounds were all bare except evergreens. Several magnolias glistened in the sun. Their leaves, dull and suedelike underneath, shone as if waxed and polished on top. The sky was clear and blue, the air like a subtle stimulant. Nature seemed to favor this venture of Mrs. Worthy's, looked on by her son and her nurse as a whim of the sick, and foolish. But maybe it wouldn't kill her, David said.

They left the driveway for bare blacktop. A short stretch of woods, then a used-car lot followed by a veterinary clinic, and they were in the city limits of Wakefield.

"Why, there's Grandpa Robbins, out raking leaves," Mrs. Worthy said, with surprise. In front of a small neat house, an old man was at work in his yard. "I thought he must be dead and buried by now."

"Oh, no." Lisa laughed. "He was in the store just recently, buying something for another grandchild."

At mention of anyone's grandchild, Mrs. Worthy always fell silent.

For weeks Lisa had neglected, to the point of ignoring, her sick mother-in-law, but with an excuse that could pass for a reason. Lisa was the bookkeeper at Worthy's, the jewelry store Mrs. Worthy's son, David, had inherited from his father, to whom it had been left by *his* father, the first D. Worthy, Jeweler, of Wakefield. Lisa was born with a talent for figures, a gift as unmistakable as perfect pitch. In childhood she liked piggy banks, coins, and numbers, not dolls. Now, with the countdown to Christmas under way, she had a new computer at the store and could almost believe her own excuses.

Mrs. Lovelady had called last night during dinner. Mrs. Worthy had announced she was going shopping today, Mrs. Lovelady said. Alone, in a taxi. Mrs. Lovelady couldn't talk her out of it, so David would have to put his foot down, she said. To solve the problem and try to redeem herself, Lisa had offered to take her.

"Want to go by the mall?" she asked, near the intersection.

"Honey, no. Thank you." Mrs. Worthy was definite. "Just one stop for me. Miss Carrie is expecting me at Hagedorn's. She said she'd have some things picked out to show me."

"What did you have in mind?"

Mrs. Worthy seemed not to hear. She was trying to find the handle to the window.

"What are you shopping for, Mrs. Worthy?" Lisa asked again, in a moment.

"Oh, a dress." Mrs. Worthy looked off to the right. "Everything I own swallows me now."

In front of a red light, Lisa looked again at her mother-in-law.

A year ago, she had seemed a different person. Off to work as a Pink Lady, gold earrings dangling from her pierced ears, she was talking, laughing, listening, busy in her church and the Charity League, running her own house. Now all that was over and Mrs. Lovelady was there, full-time. Behind them a bearded black man blew the horn of a Datsun. The light had turned green.

"Miss Carrie could have sent some things out," Lisa said, moving into the proper lane. "You could have tried them at home."

"But somebody would have to take them back, maybe try again. No, this will be easier. On everybody."

"Well, we have a beautiful day," Lisa said, with a smile.

It would be good to tell people, constantly asking, that she had seen Mrs. Worthy and had taken her shopping. "She's doing better, gaining a little weight," David had been saying lately, and she'd been repeating. Actually, Mrs. Worthy was no better at all and, if anything, worse.

Most of what David said Lisa didn't repeat. Health reports aside, it was the same in effect. His mother was a hero.

He had always praised her. "When we got home from school, she was there," he would say. Or, "Nobody could make hot rolls or mayonnaise like she could." Now his praise was on a different plane and Lisa heard it daily, her mother-in-law's courage, stoicism, self-sacrifice. After a day at the store, she heard it at night as she worked in the kitchen. Usually, she listened in silence.

"What do you mean, 'sacrifice'?" The words popped out one night, to her own surprise. "She has everything anybody could want."

His job was setting the table. Beside the sterling flatware he put down paper napkins. At first he said nothing, then his answer came like a blow in slow motion. "Not quite," he said, estranged already for several days to come. "She's sick, with nobody to look after her but a paid companion."

His mother came first with David, Lisa felt. She had thought so from the start, or almost the start. There had been a short happy time before she began to suspect that Mrs. Worthy sat on his right hand and she, Lisa, somewhere on the left. When she finally said so, in a burst of frustration, he was amazed.

"But she's alone now, and she's my mother!" he protested. "I love you both. Don't you know that?"

She didn't care about both. It was not to be shared. Something inside her was always watching for, ready to resist, any such notion on anyone's part.

David still referred to his mother's house as home, to their own home as "the house." "I'll run by home and see Mama, then meet you at the house," he began to say each afternoon as Mrs. Worthy grew worse. He also ran by on his way to work in the morning, and sometimes during lunch.

Mrs. Worthy was not to blame, Lisa knew. The bond had been forged too long ago and had nothing to do with her. Besides, Mrs. Worthy asked for nothing. On the contrary, she gave so much Lisa didn't like the obligations involved. Mrs. Worthy was a "giver," people said.

Once the three of them had gone to church together, a weekly habit. At the family pew, Mrs. Worthy stood back for Lisa to enter first. When David in turn stood back for his mother, she motioned him ahead of her to sit by Lisa. Sunday after Sunday he sat between them, his eyes on the preacher with polite disinterest. Sunlight, coming through a stained-glass window, fell on him like a halo. His face between them, in that light, was fixed in Lisa's mind forever, she thought.

Hagedorn's, like Worthy's, had been family owned for three generations. Lisa preferred Lowe's, which had a younger, newer clientele; but Mrs. Worthy did most of her shopping at Hagedorn's, and had for forty years. Lisa was relieved to find a parking place in front. When she came around to help Mrs. Worthy out, her mother-in-law was trying this time to find the handle to the door.

"I'm a real drag now, Lisa," she said.

Lisa wondered where she got the word, *drag*. Not from grandchildren that she wanted so much, and didn't have. Of the children she had brought into the world, only David was living. Her daughter had been killed in a teenage wreck, her other son in Vietnam. Now, since no one could take Lisa's place at the store, she and David were putting off children as long as possible, maybe altogether. They no longer even discussed it. Lisa had left the Catholic church and its birth-control laws. The Worthy family had been Baptist for generations, Southern Baptists, as unyielding on dogma as Catholics themselves. Lisa, a cradle Catholic, had felt she should join them.

"You'd give up your *soul* for him?" her father had asked, stunned, when she told him her decision. Later, in Wakefield, people would say, "She worships him." She should love her husband a reasonable amount, they seemed to think, and spread the rest around (family, friends, a good cause or hobby). When, in eight years, she had played no bridge, produced no child, joined no clique or club, they gave up on her. She was simply David Worthy's wife, "a girl from up north somewhere."

The windows of Hagedorn's were ready for Christmas, with formals and furs on one side, lingerie and robes on the other. While waiting for Mrs. Worthy to turn in her seat, to put one foot out and then the other, Lisa studied the display. Nice but dull, in her opinion. Nothing exciting in the least. The truth was, David carried out a similar policy at Worthy's. Lenox, Gorham, Waterford, diamonds in Tiffany settings. Lisa would like to add a little Steuben glass, a few pieces of costume jewelry by Dior or Chanel. Anything new and different, but no. "It wouldn't go over, love," he said. "This is Wakefield. And Worthy's."

Mrs. Worthy took a few steps, holding to Lisa's arm, and had to stop.

"Want to go back?" Lisa asked.

"No, give me a minute."

To avoid the looks of passersby, Lisa fixed her attention on the cane Mrs. Worthy leaned on. She had seen it before in Mrs. Worthy's back-hall closet, one of several left behind by members of the family. Someone's initials were engraved on the band, but all Lisa could make out was a central *W* through which other letters looped. When Mrs. Worthy first had to take over the big house and all the family relics, it was the last thing on earth she wanted to do, she once told Lisa. She had considered herself only an in-law at the time, she said. Now she took a deep breath and, still holding Lisa's arm, began to walk.

In the store everyone came up to greet her with hugs and handclasps. Everyone wanted to touch her, it seemed. On Lisa's arm, her hand began to tremble.

"Thank you all, thank you." Her eyes filled with tears, but she rallied. "It's so good to see you! How *are* you?"

Lisa wouldn't have known the strain she was under, except for the telltale grip on her arm. She herself did not aspire to such grace. She was from Chicago, the daughter of an Irish contractor, successful, but self-made. When her mother died, he'd sent her to Catholic boarding schools and finally, against her wishes, to a sheltered college for women, near Wakefield. Sometimes at night, in the poster bed from David's old bedroom, the whole thing seemed more dream than reality— the Deep South like a foreign country, the Worthys with their contradictory piety and pride, the big house that was more than a house. Sometimes even David, behind the façade of manners and codes. Everything but the store, where surrounded by accounts and figures she felt at home.

As a new wife, she had wanted a new bed and had impulsively bought one, king-size, with her own money. David didn't say so, but she knew he wasn't thrilled. "We don't need all this room," he finally said. "Do we? I want you closer." She had put an ad in the paper and sold the bed, new bedclothes, all.

The elevator operator, a black woman, made Mrs. Worthy laugh as they went up. "Pretty as ever," the black woman said. "Go buy you one them fur coats out the window!"

Miss Carrie, on the third floor, was a stout strawberry blonde, the color of her hair a little hectic today. In navy blue over a snug foundation, she was watching for her old customer when the elevator door opened. At first sight of Mrs. Worthy, the muscles of her face went slack, but she came forward smiling.

"Bless your sweet heart!" She took Mrs. Worthy's arm. "I'm so glad to see you. Let's go sit down."

Facing the elevator, near the center of the floor, a place was set aside for customers to wait, rest, and visit. Sofas and chairs were grouped around an Oriental rug. Tables held lamps and ashtrays, sometimes a potted plant or flowers from someone's garden. The spot, comfortable as the living room of a friend, was seldom without someone sitting there, purses and packages lying about.

Mrs. Worthy decided on a chair to sit in, and Miss Carrie turned to Lisa. "I'll take her now," she said, to Lisa's surprise.

"Yes, Lisa." Propped on her cane, Mrs. Worthy agreed. "Miss Carrie will help me. Thank you for getting me up here, my dear."

Lisa was dismissed. That she understood. Was she also being censured? Did everyone know she had not been attentive? Southerners were masters of indirection, she had found.

"When do you want me back?" she asked cautiously.

"Before long, I'm afraid." Mrs. Worthy swapped her cane for Miss Carrie's arm, and began the process of sitting down.

The black woman shook her head when the door was shut. "Lord, Lord," she said mournfully. "She going down fast now, and she so nice. I loves that lady."

Lisa knew what to say, but she stared at the floor and said nothing. No one could see her side at all, she thought, much less understand. So why care? In front of the store she checked her watch and, knowing she probably shouldn't, hurried down to Lowe's.

Lowe's too was ready for Christmas. Against a background of black and silver, like a starry night, one window featured evening gowns in shimmering holiday colors. Beaded, embroidered, winking with sequins. The spotlight, however, was on white, a crepe dress on a dais near the center of the window. Simple and Grecian, it was draped to one side and caught on the shoulder with a rhinestone clip, leaving the other shoulder deeply bare.

Ah! Lisa needed something new for the big Christmas dance. She had seen and liked the dress in a magazine, had even considered ordering it by phone. What a coincidence to find it at Lowe's! The only one, they said, but in her size, and if she would wait, they'd get it from the window.

Lisa's regular salesgirl was off today. The one who brought the dress, whose name she didn't know, had large blue-green eyes, dramatically made up with lids like green satin. In a dressing room, she helped Lisa get the dress on, then stepped back to view it.

"You look like something for the top of the tree," she said.

Lisa studied her reflection in the mirror. The dressing room lights put an overlay of gold on her medium-blond hair and skin. In white she did suggest, remotely, a certain concept of angel. But the dress was really Greek, its true association with broken columns and sculpture with blind, unfinished eyes.

"I want you to see that back, see the whole thing," the salesgirl said. With a motion like windshield wipers, her girdled hips led the way to a three-way mirror out on the floor.

In front of the mirrors a stylish older woman stood smoking, trying to make up her mind about a navy blue blazer she had on. She moved aside but not away and, with shaky fingers, raised the cigarette to her lips. While she exhaled, she looked at Lisa.

"That dress is out of this world on you," she said, coughing and choking. Ashes fell on her gray shoes like suede on suede.

David didn't always care for her clothes, Lisa knew, in spite of her efforts to please him. This time, for once, she was sure. He would love her in the white dress. She knew exactly how his eyes would look as he walked into the ballroom with her. The material, subtly draped, was as soft and light as air, the price more than she'd ever paid for a dress in her life.

"Think of it this way," the salesgirl said, as she helped take it off. "How can you afford *not* to get it?"

"I know." Lisa laughed. "I'd pay in regret, wouldn't I?"

She glanced at her watch, slipped on her skirt, and left the dressing room still buttoning her blouse.

The salesgirl was folding the dress for a large pink box with LOWE's in lipstick-red on the top. "Want this charged?" she asked.

"Yes, please, I'm Lisa Worthy. My husband . . ."

"Oh, I know. I know Mrs. Worthy senior. How is she?"

"Not well at all." Lisa waited at the desk. "I'm on my way to pick her up now, and I'm late."

"Everybody in town is pulling for her," the salesgirl said, working faster. "She's such a doll, it's just not fair. Well . . ." She handed the box to Lisa. "Thank you. Have a nice day."

Lisa hurried to the car and put the box out of sight in the trunk, so Mrs. Worthy wouldn't see it. Guilt, she supposed. Always guilt. Guilt on top of guilt. What she needed was to go to confession, and a wave of loss swept over her. She thought with longing of her rosary and missal and wondered where she had put them. She would hunt them up and use them. No one would know, and what if they did? At the thought, guilt gave way to resentment, toward what or whom she didn't even know.

In Hagedorn's she had to wait for the elevator, then got on alone. The operator, usually friendly and chatty, had nothing to say. Lisa hoped Miss Carrie, or somebody, had been looking after Mrs. Worthy. She would be worn out from waiting, but she'd be nice about it. They could go straight home and get it over.

When the door rattled open, she felt a deepening chill. Mrs. Worthy was asleep on a sofa, her chin on her chest, her hat askew. Beside her was a pearl-gray dress box.

Miss Carrie came forward with a swish of nylon-clad legs rubbing against one another. "She had to take a pain pill," Miss Carrie said, like an accusation. "It knocked her right out."

Lisa said nothing. Having hoped in vain for the best, she was not prepared for this. Like a target moving toward the arrow, she approached her mother-in-law in silence. Every eye on the third floor was upon her, she knew.

"Mrs. Worthy?" she said softly, leaning down.

Mrs. Worthy opened her eyes and held up her head. She looked from Lisa and Miss Carrie to racks of skirts and blouses, then walls lined with clothing beyond. "Oh, me, me, me," she said, pulling herself together. "Are we through?"

"Through, and had a nice little nap besides." Miss Carrie was breathing too fast. A pulse beat hard in the lap of her throat.

"I've come to take you home," Lisa said. "When you're ready."

Mrs. Worthy sighed. Her hands began to feel around for her purse.

"I have your things, ladylove," Miss Carrie held out the purse and cane. "I'll carry them down for you. Want a sip of coffee first? Would that taste good?"

Mrs. Worthy shook her head and Lisa wondered what to do about the hat, ludicrous at that angle. When she presumed to fix it, Mrs. Worthy paid no attention, like a child having its headgear adjusted.

"Ready?" Lisa picked up the dress box.

Mrs. Worthy had to be supported to the elevator, where the black woman averted her eyes and worked the controls in silence. Mrs. Worthy leaned on Miss Carrie, who kept one arm around her waist. Lisa stared blindly at advertisements taped to the wall, wondering what vanity or pride could prompt anyone so sick to subject herself, subject them all, to such an ordeal.

When the elevator stopped, Miss Carrie looked past Mrs. Worthy to Lisa. "I'll go on to the car with you," she said.

"Watch your step," the black woman cautioned.

Mrs. Worthy was plainly in no condition for farewells, and no one on the main floor approached her. The three women went slowly by a selection of nightgowns rising up as on kneeling ghosts above a long glass counter, their lace-trimmed hems arranged in swirls around them. They passed robes and caftans, slips and bras. Handbags lined a portion of the wall on their left, and a faint scent of leather hovered about. After costume jewelry and scarves, they finally reached the front. Someone was on hand to open the heavy double doors.

At the car Lisa and Miss Carrie lowered Mrs. Worthy backward into the seat. Lisa picked up her mother-in-law's legs, set them in place, and shut the car door. Outside the raised window, Miss Carrie tapped the glass and waved. Mrs. Worthy gave her a blank smile like a check she'd forgotten to sign, and sank back in the seat.

Lisa put down the windows and let in a rush of fresh air. Mrs. Worthy came to, to a degree.

"Those new pills are too strong," she said, frowning. "They put me to sleep sitting up."

Like the fullness of indigestion, Lisa's conscience rose up. She should take the blame and apologize, she knew; but she turned her head, let the wind blow her hair the other way, and said nothing.

"Did you find a dress you liked?" she asked, when the moment had passed.

Mrs. Worthy looked out the window. "I hope so," she said.

"It didn't have to be altered?"

"No, I decided not to bother."

Sick, sick, Lisa thought. Before, everything had to be right. For a quarter of an inch, a hem would be taken up or let down. Clothes had to fit but with ease; not too loose, but never tight.

The sun, straight overhead, fixed a blinding headlight on the windshield of each approaching car. Lisa lowered the visors on both sides, though Mrs. Worthy seemed not to mind the glare and stared ahead as if immune to it. Grandpa Robbins was no longer to be seen in the big yard he kept with such determination.

Beyond a wall of trees, mostly bare, the house came into view. Ready for the next hundred years, Lisa thought. For the rest of her life. She fixed her attention resolutely on the road. This time she drove on to the back, where the door would be closer, steps fewer, and came to a careful stop. Mrs. Worthy's Irish setter, Missy, was barking to announce them, so Mrs. Lovelady would be out to help any minute.

"Home again," Lisa said, with relief. Mrs. Worthy smiled and said nothing. All morning Lisa had wondered at her patience, like that of the poor, who could sit and wait for hours. An effect of the pills, she supposed. She turned to the box on the backseat.

"Mind if I look?"

For a split second, Mrs. Worthy didn't answer. It was as if a burst of glare to which she was not immune had suddenly struck her in the face. "Of course not," she said, when it passed.

Lisa held the box between them and lifted the top, then the crisp tissue paper. To her surprise she saw crepe de chine with tucks and lace, in a dusky shade of rose. She'd been expecting something else, an ordinary dress for trips to the doctor.

"Beautiful," she said, impressed but puzzled.

"We used to call that color 'ashes of roses.'" Mrs. Worthy gave a quick, light laugh. Humor flared up in her eyes like small flames.

A vision of absolute stillness flashed before Lisa, the rose dress on a background of tufted white satin. Staring at Mrs. Worthy, she felt the blood drain from her face while her heart seemed to rise up and flop over like a large fish. In the open box, tissue paper waved and shook from the trembling of her hands.

She knew that Mrs. Lovelady had appeared off to one side, that Mrs. Lovelady was speaking, perhaps to her. Unable to respond, as in a nightmare, she went on staring at her mother-in-law as if she'd never seen her before, as if what she saw was not a face but a revelation, not to be taken in all at once, in the blinking of an eye.

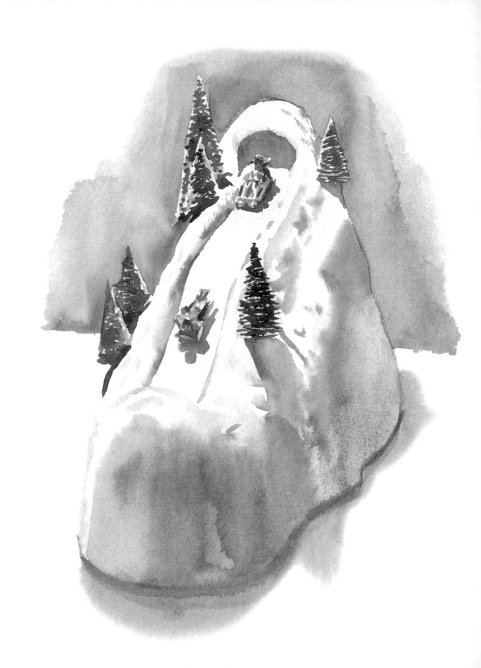

Crèche

by Richard Ford

Faith is not driving them; her mother, Esther, is.

In the car, it's the five of them. The family, on their way to Snow Mountain Highlands, to ski. Sandusky, Ohio, to northern Michigan. It's Christmas, or nearly. No one wants to spend Christmas alone.

The five include Faith, who's the motion-picture lawyer, arrived from California; her mother, Esther, who's sixty-four and has, over the years, become much too fat. There's Roger, Faith's sister Daisy's estranged husband, a guidance counselor at Sandusky JFK; and Roger's two girls, Jane and Marjorie, ages eight and six. Daisy— the girls' mom—is a presence, but not along. She's in rehab in a large midwestern city that is not Chicago or Detroit.

Outside, beyond the long, treeless expanse of whitely frozen winterscape, Lake Michigan itself becomes suddenly visible, pale blue with a thin veneer of fog just above its metallic surface. The girls are chatting in the backseat. Roger is beside them reading *Skier* magazine.

Florida would've been a much nicer holiday alternative, Faith thinks. Epcot for the girls. The Space Center. Satellite Beach. Fresh pompano. The ocean. She's paying for everything and doesn't even like to ski. But it's been a hard year for everyone, and somebody has to take charge. If they'd gone to Florida, she'd have ended up broke.

Her basic character strength, Faith thinks, watching what seems to be a nuclear power plant coming up on the left, is the same feature that makes her a first-rate lawyer: an undeterrable willingness to see things as capable of being made better, and an addiction to thoroughness. If someone at the studio, a VP in marketing, for example, wishes to exit from a totally binding yet surprisingly uncomfortable obligation—say, a legal contract—then Faith's your girl. Faith the doer. Faith the blond beauty with smarts. Your very own optimist. A client's dream with great tits. Her own tits. Just give her a day on your problem.

Her sister Daisy is the perfect case in point. Daisy has been able to admit her serious methamphetamine problem, but only after her biker boyfriend, Vince, had been made a guest of the state of Ohio. And here Faith has had a role to play, beginning with phone calls to attorneys, a restraining order, then later the police and handcuffs for Vince. Daisy, strung out and thoroughly bruised, finally proved to be a credible witness, once convinced she would not be killed.

Going through Daisy's apartment with their mother, in search of clothes Daisy could wear with dignity into rehab, Faith found dildos; six in all—one even under the kitchen sink. These she put in a plastic Grand Union bag and left in the neighbor's street garbage just so her mother wouldn't know. Her mother is up-to-date, but not necessarily interested in dildos. For Daisy's going-in outfit, they eventually settled on a nice, dark jersey shift and some new white Adidas.

The downside of the character issue, the nonlawyer side, Faith understands, is the fact that she's almost thirty-seven and nothing's very solid in her life. She is very patient (with assholes), very good to help behind the scenes (with assholes). Her glass is always half full. Stand and Ameliorate could be her motto. Anticipate change. The skills of the law, again, only partly in sync with the requirements of life.

A tall silver smokestack with blinking white lights on top and several gray megaphone-shaped cooling pots around it now passes on the left. Dense, chalky smoke drifts out of each pot. Lake Michigan, beyond, looks like a blue-white desert. It has snowed for three days, but has stopped now.

"What's that big thing?" Jane or possibly Marjorie says, peering out the backseat window. It is too warm in the cranberry-colored Suburban Faith rented at the Cleveland airport especially for the trip. The girls are both chewing watermelon-smelling gum. Everyone could get carsick.

"That's a rocket ship ready to blast off to outer space. Would you girls like to hitch a ride on it?" Roger, the brother-in-law, says to his daughters. Roger is the friendly funny neighbor in a family sitcom, although not that funny. He is small and blandly handsome and wears a brush cut and black horn-rimmed glasses. And he is loathsome—though in subtle ways, like some TV actors Faith has known. He is also thirty-seven and prefers pastel cardigans and Hush Puppies. Daisy has been very, very unfaithful to him.

"It is *not* a rocket ship," says Jane, the older child, putting her forehead to the foggy window, then pulling back to consider the smudge mark she's left.

"It's a pickle," Marjorie says.

"And shut up," Jane says. "That's a nasty expression."

"No it's not," Marjorie says.

"Is that a word your mother taught you?" Roger asks and smirks. He is in the backseat with them. "I bet it is. That's her legacy. Pickle." On the cover of *Skier* is a photograph of Hermann Maier, wearing an electric-red outfit, slaloming down Mount Everest. The headline says, GOING TO EXTREMES.

"It better not be," Faith's mother says from behind the wheel. She has her seat pushed way back to accommodate her stomach.

"Okay. Two more guesses," Roger says.

"It's an atom plant where they make electricity," Faith says, and smiles back at the nieces, who are staring out at the smokestacks, losing interest. "We use it to heat our houses."

"But we don't like them," Esther says. Esther's been green since before it was chic.

"Why?" Jane says.

"Because they threaten our precious environment, that's why," Esther answers.

"What's 'our precious environment'?" Jane says insincerely.

"The air we breathe, the ground we stand on, the water we drink."
Once Esther taught eighth-grade science, but not in years.

"Don't you girls learn anything in school?" Roger is flipping pages in his *Skier*. For some mysterious reason, Faith has noticed, Roger is quite tanned.

"Their father could always instruct them," Esther says. "He's in education."

"Guidance," Roger says. "But touché."

"What's touché?" Jane says, wrinkling her nose.

"It's a term used in fencing," Faith says. She likes both girls immensely, and would happily punish Roger for speaking to them with sarcasm.

"What's fencing," Marjorie asks.

"It's a town in Michigan where they make fences," Roger says. "Fencing, Michigan. It's near Lansing."

"No it's not," Faith says.

"Well, then, you tell them," Roger says. "You know everything. You're the lawyer."

"It's a game you play with swords," Faith says. "Only no one gets killed. It's fun." In every respect, she despises Roger and wishes he'd stayed in Sandusky. But she couldn't ask the little girls without him. Letting her pay for everything is Roger's way of saying thanks.

"So. There you are, little girls. You heard it here first," Roger says in a nice-nasty voice, continuing to read. "All your lives now you'll remember where you heard fencing explained first and by whom. When you're at Harvard . . ."

"You didn't know," Jane says.

"That's wrong. I did know. I absolutely knew," Roger says. "I was just having some fun. Christmas is a fun time, don't you know?"

FAITH'S LOVE LIFE has not been going well. She has always wanted children-with-marriage, but neither of these things has quite happened. Either the men she's liked haven't liked children, or else the men who loved her and wanted to give her all she longed for haven't seemed worth it. Practicing law for a movie studio has therefore become very engrossing. Time has gone by. A series of mostly courteous men has entered but then departed—all for one reason or another unworkable: married, frightened, divorced, all three together. "Lucky" is how she has chiefly seen herself. She goes to the gym every day, drives an expensive car, lives alone in Venice Beach in a rental owned by a teenage movie star who is a friend's brother and who has HIV. A deal.

Late last spring she met a man. A stock market hotsy-totsy with a house on Nantucket. Jack. Jack flew to Nantucket from the city in his own plane, had never been married at age roughly forty-six. She came east a few times and flew up with him, met his stern-looking sisters, the pretty, socialite mom. There was a big blue rambling beach house facing the sea, with rose hedges, sandy pathways to secret dunes where you could swim naked—something she especially enjoyed, though the sisters were astounded. The father was there, but was sick and would soon die, so life and plans were generally on hold. Jack did beaucoup business in London. Money was not a problem. Maybe when the father departed they could be married, Jack had almost suggested. But until then, she could travel with him whenever she could get away—scale back a little on the expectation side. He wanted children, could get to California often. It could work.

One night a woman called. Greta, she said her name was. Greta was in love with Jack. She and Jack had had a fight, but he still loved her, she said. It turned out Greta had pictures of Faith and Jack together. Who knew who took them? A little bird. One was a picture of Faith and Jack exiting Jack's building on Beekman Place. Another was of Jack helping Faith out of a yellow taxi. One was of Faith, alone, at the Park Avenue Café eating seared swordfish. One was of Jack and Faith kissing in the front seat of an unrecognizable car—also in New York.

Jack liked particular kinds of sex in very particular kinds of ways, Greta said on the phone. She guessed Faith knew all about that by now. But "best not make long-range plans" was somehow the message. Other calls were placed, messages left on her voice mail, prints arrived by FedEx.

When asked, Jack conceded there was a problem. But he would solve it, *tout de suite* (though she needed to understand he was preoccupied with his father's approaching death). Jack was a tall, smooth-faced, handsome man with a chock of lustrous, mahogany-colored hair. Like a clothing model. He smiled and everyone felt better. He'd gone to public high school, Harvard, played squash, rowed, debated, looked good in a brown suit and oldish shoes. He was trustworthy. It still seemed workable.

But Greta called more times. She sent pictures of herself and Jack together. Recent pictures, since Faith had come on board. It was harder than he'd imagined to get untangled, Jack admitted. Faith would need to be patient. Greta was, after all, someone he'd once "cared about very much." Might've even married. Didn't wish to hurt. She had problems, yes. But he wouldn't just throw her over. He wasn't that kind of man, something she, Faith, would be glad about in the long run. Meanwhile, there was the sick patriarch. And his mother. And the sisters. That had been plenty.

Snow Mountain Highlands is a smaller ski resort, but nice. Family, not flash. Faith's mother found it as a "Holiday Get-away" in the *Erie Weekly*. The package includes a condo, weekend lift tickets, and coupons for three days of Swedish smorgasbord in the Bavarian-style lodge. The deal, however, is for two people only. The rest have to pay. Faith will sleep with her mother in the "Master Suite." Roger can share the twin with the girls.

Two years ago, when sister Daisy began to take an interest in Vince, the biker, Roger simply "receded." Her and Roger's sex life had long ago lost its effervescence, Daisy confided. They had started off well enough as a model couple in a suburb of Sandusky, but eventually—after some years and two kids—happiness ended and Daisy had been won over by Vince, who liked amphetamines and more importantly sold them. Vince's arrival was when sex had gotten really good, Daisy said. Faith believes Daisy envied her movie connections and movie lifestyle and the Jaguar convertible and basically threw her own life away (at least until rehab) as a way of simulating Faith's, only with a biker. Eventually Daisy left home and gained forty-five pounds on a body that was already voluptuous, if short. Last summer, at the beach at Middle Bass, Daisy in a rage actually punched Faith in the chest when she suggested that Daisy might lose some weight, ditch Vince, and consider coming home to her family. Not a diplomatic suggestion, she later decided. "I'm not like you," Daisy screamed, right out on the sandy beach. "I fuck for pleasure. Not for business." Then she waddled into the tepid surf of Lake Erie, wearing a pink one-piece that boasted a frilly skirtlet. By then, Roger had the girls, courtesy of a court order.

IN THE CONDO NOW, Esther has been watching her soaps, but has stopped to play double solitaire and have a glass of wine by the big picture window that looks down toward the crowded ski slope and the ice rink. Roger is actually there on the bunny slope with Jane and Marjorie, though it's impossible to distinguish them. Red suits. Yellow suits. Lots of dads with kids. All of it soundless.

Faith has had a sauna and is now thinking about phoning Jack, wherever Jack is. Nantucket. New York. London. She has no particular message to leave. Later she plans to do the Nordic Trail under moonlight. Just to be a full participant, to set a good example.

For this she has brought L.A. purchases: loden knickers, a green-and-brown-and-red sweater knitted in the Himalayas, socks from Norway. No way does she plan to get cold.

Esther plays cards at high speed with two decks, her short fat fingers flipping cards and snapping them down as if she hates the game and wants it to be over. Her eyes are intent. She has put on a cream-colored neck brace because the tension of driving has aggravated an old work-related injury. And she is now wearing a big Hawaii-print orange muumuu. How long, Faith wonders, has she been wearing these tents? Twenty years, at least. Since Faith's own father—Esther's husband—kicked the bucket.

"Maybe I'll go to Europe," Esther says, flicking cards ferociously. "That'd be nice, wouldn't it?"

Faith is at the window, observing the expert slope. Smooth, wide pastures of snow, framed by copses of beautiful spruces. Several skiers are zigzagging their way down, doing their best to appear stylish. Years ago, she came here with her high-school boyfriend, Eddie, a.k.a. "Fast Eddie," which in some respects he was. Neither of them liked to ski, nor did they get out of bed to try. Now, skiing reminds her of golf—a golf course made of snow.

"Maybe I'll take the girls out of school and treat us all to Venice," Esther goes on. "I'm sure Roger would be relieved."

Faith has spotted Roger and the girls on the bunny slope. Blue, green and yellow suits, respectively. He is pointing, giving detailed instructions to his daughters about ski etiquette. Just like any dad.

She thinks she sees him laughing. It is hard to think of Roger as an average parent.

"They're too young for Venice," Faith says, putting her small, good-looking nose near the surprisingly warm windowpane. From outside, she hears the rasp of a snow shovel and muffled voices.

"Maybe I'll take *you* to Europe, then," Esther says. "Maybe when Daisy clears rehab we can all three take in Europe. I always planned for that."

Faith likes her mother. Her mother is no fool, yet still seeks ways to be generous. But Faith cannot complete a picture that includes herself, her enlarged mother, and Daisy on the Champs-Elysées or the Grand Canal. "That's a nice idea," she says. She is standing beside her mother's chair, looking down at the top of her head, hearing her breathe. Her mother's head is small. Its hair is dark gray and short and sparse, and not especially clean. She has affected a very wide part straight down the middle. Her mother looks like the fat lady in the circus, but wearing a neck brace.

"I was reading what it takes to live to a hundred," Esther says, neatening the cards on the glass table top in front of her belly. Faith has begun thinking of Jack and what a peculiar species of creep he is. Jack Matthews still wears the Lobb cap-toe shoes he had made for him in college. Ugly, pretentious English shoes. "You have to be physically active," her mother continues. "And you have to be an optimist, which I am. You have to stay interested in things, which I more or less do. And you have to handle loss well."

With all her concentration Faith tries not to wonder how she ranks on this scale. "Do you want to be a hundred?"

"Oh, yes," her mother says. "*You* just can't imagine it, that's all. You're too young. And beautiful. And talented." No irony. Irony is not her mother's specialty.

Outside, one of the men shoveling snow can be heard to say, "Hi, we're the Weather Channel." He's speaking to someone watching them through another window from yet another condo.

"Colder'n a well-digger's dick, you bet," a second man's voice says. "That's today's forecast."

"Dicks, dicks, and more dicks," her mother says pleasantly. "That's it, isn't it? The male appliance. The whole mystery."

"So I'm told," Faith says, and thinks about Fast Eddie.

"They were all women, though," her mother says.

"Who?"

"All the people who lived to be a hundred. You could do all the other things right. But you still needed to be a woman to survive."

"Good for us," Faith says.

"Right. The lucky few."

THIS WILL BE THE girls' first Christmas without a tree or their mother. Though Faith has attempted to improvise around this by arranging presents at the base of the large, plastic rubber-tree plant stationed against one of the empty white walls of the small living room. The tree was already here. She has brought with her a few Christmas balls, a gold star, and a string of lights that promise to blink. "Christmas in Manila" could be a possible theme.

Outside, the day is growing dim. Faith's mother is napping. Following his ski lesson, Roger has gone down to The Warming Shed for a mulled wine. The girls are seated on the couch side by side, wearing their Lanz of Salzburg flannel nighties with matching smiling monkey-face slippers. They have taken their baths together, with Faith to supervise, then insisted on putting on their nighties early for their nap. They seem perfect angels and perfectly wasted on their parents. Faith has decided to pay their college tuitions. Even to Harvard.

"We know how to ski now," Jane says primly. They're watching Faith trim the plastic rubber-tree plant. First the blinking lights, though there's no plug-in close enough, then the six balls (one for each family member). Last will come the gold star. Faith understands she is trying for too much. Though why not try for too much. It's Christmas. "Marjorie wants to go to the Olympics," Jane adds.

Jane has watched the Olympics on TV, but Marjorie was too young. It is Jane's power position. Marjorie looks at her sister without expression, as if no one can observe her staring.

"I'm sure she'll win a medal," Faith says, on her knees, fiddling with the fragile strand of tiny peaked bulbs she already knows will not light up. "Would you two like to help me?" She smiles at both of them.

"No," Jane says.

"No," Marjorie says immediately after.

"I don't blame you," Faith says.

"Is Mommy coming here?" Marjorie blinks, then crosses her tiny, pale ankles. She is sleepy and could possibly cry.

"No, sweet," Faith says. "This Christmas Mommy is doing *herself* a favor. So she can't do one for us."

"What about Vince?" Jane says authoritatively. Vince is ground that has been gone over several times before now, and carefully. Mrs. Argenbright, the girls' therapist, has taken special pains with the Vince subject. The girls have the skinny on Mr. Vince but want to be given it again, since they like Vince more than their father.

"Vince is a guest of the state of Ohio, right now," Faith says. "You remember that? It's like he's in college."

"He's not in college," Jane says.

"Does he have a tree where he is?" Marjorie asks.

"Not in any real sense, at least not in his room like you do," Faith says. "Let's talk about happier things than our friend Vince, okay?" She is stringing bulbs now, on her knees.

The room doesn't include much furniture, and what there is conforms to the Danish modern style. A raised, metal-hooded, red-enamel fireplace device has a paper message from the condo owners taped to it, advising that smoke damage will cause renters to lose their security deposit and subject them to legal actions. These particular owners, Esther has learned, are residents of Grosse Pointe Farms and are people of Russian extraction. There's, of course, no firewood except what the Danish furniture could offer. So smoke is unlikely. Baseboards supply everything.

"I think you two should guess what you're getting for Christmas," Faith says, carefully draping lightless lights onto the stiff plastic branches of the rubber tree. Taking pains.

"In-lines. I already know," Jane says and crosses her ankles like her sister. They are a jury disguised as an audience. "I don't have to wear a helmet, though."

"But are your sure of that?" Faith glances over her shoulder and gives them a smile she's seen movie stars give to strangers. "You could always be wrong."

"I'd better be right," Jane says unpleasantly, with a frown very much like her mom's.

"Santa's bringing me a disc player," Marjorie says. "It'll come in a small box. I won't even recognize it."

"You two're too smart for your britches," Faith says. She is quickly finished stringing Christmas lights. "But you don't know what *I* brought you." Among other things, she has brought a disc player and an expensive pair of in-line skates. They are in the Suburban and will be returned back in L.A. She has also brought movie videos. Twenty in all, including *Star Wars* and *Sleeping Beauty*. Daisy has sent them each fifty dollars.

"You know," Faith says, "I remember once a long, long time ago, my dad and I and your mom went out in the woods and cut a tree for Christmas. We didn't buy a tree, we cut one down with an axe."

Jane and Marjorie stare at her as if they've read this story some-place. The TV is not turned on in the room. Perhaps, Faith thinks, they don't understand someone talking to them—live action pre-senting its own unique continuity problems.

"Do you want to hear the story?"

"Yes," Marjorie, the younger sister, says. Jane sits watchful and silent on the green Danish sofa. Behind her on the bare white wall is a framed print of Brueghel's *Return of the Hunters*, which is, af-ter all, Christmas-y.

"Well," Faith says. "Your mother and I—we were only nine and ten—picked out the tree we desperately wanted to be our tree, but our dad said no, that tree was too tall to fit inside our house. We should choose another one. But we both said, 'No, this one's per-fect. This is the best one.' It was green and pretty and had a perfect Christmas shape. So our dad cut it down with his axe, and we dragged it out through the woods and tied it on top of our car and brought it back to Sandusky." Both girls are sleepy now. There has been too much excitement, or else not enough. Their mother is in rehab. Their dad's an asshole. They're in someplace called Michi-gan. Who wouldn't be sleepy?

"Do you want to know what happened after that?" Faith says. "When we got the tree inside?"

"Yes," Marjorie says politely.

"It *was* too big," Faith says. "It was much, much too tall. It couldn't even stand up in our living room. And it was too wide. And our dad got really mad at us because we'd killed a beautiful living tree for a selfish reason, and because we hadn't listened to him and thought we knew everything just because we knew what we wanted."

Faith suddenly doesn't know why she's telling this story to these innocent sweeties who do not need another object lesson. So she simply stops. In the real story, of course, her father took the tree and threw it out the door into the backyard, where it stayed for a week and turned brown. There was crying and accusations. Her father went straight to a bar and got drunk. Later, their mother went to the Kiwanis lot and bought a small tree that fit and that the three of them trimmed without the aid of their father. It was waiting, all lighted, when he came home smashed. The story had always been one others found humor in. This time the humor seems lacking.

"Do you want to know how the story turned out?" Faith says, smiling brightly for the girls' benefit, but feeling defeated.

"I do," Marjorie says. Jane says nothing.

"Well, we put it outside in the yard and put lights on it so our neighbors could share our big tree with us. And we bought a smaller tree for the house at the Kiwanis. It was a sad story that turned out good."

"I don't believe that," Jane says.

"Well you should believe it," Faith says, "because it's true. Christmases are special. They always turn out wonderfully if you just give them a chance and use your imagination."

Jane shakes her head as Marjorie nods hers. Marjorie wants to believe. Jane, Faith thinks, is a classic older child. Like herself.

"Did you know"—this was one of Greta's cute messages left for her on her voice mail in Los Angeles—"did you know that Jack hates—*hates*—to have his dick sucked? Hates it with a passion. Of course you didn't. How could you? He always lies about it. Oh well. But if you're wondering why he never comes, that's why. It's a big turn-off for him. I personally think it's his mother's fault, not that *she* ever did it to him, of course. By the way, that was a nice dress last Friday. Really great tits. I can see why Jack likes you. Take care."

At seven, when the girls wake up from their naps and everyone is hungry at once, Faith's mother offers to take the two hostile Indians for a pizza, then on to the skating rink, while Roger and Faith share the smorgasbord coupons in the lodge.

Very few diners have chosen the long, harshly lit, rather sour-smelling Tyrol Room. Most guests are outside awaiting the Pageant of Lights, in which members of the ski patrol descend the expert slope each night holding flaming torches. It is a thing of beauty but takes time getting started. At the very top of the hill a giant Norway spruce has been illuminated in the Yuletide tradition, just as in the untrue version of Faith's story. All of this is viewable from inside the Tyrol Room via a great picture window.

Faith does not want to eat with Roger, who is hungover from his *Glühwein* and a nap. Conversation that she would find offensive could easily occur; something on the subject of her sister, the girls' mother—Roger's (still) wife. But she's trying to keep up a Christmas spirit. Do for others, etc.

Roger, she knows, dislikes her, possibly envies her, and also is attracted to her. Once, several years ago, he confided to her that he'd very much like to fuck her ears flat. He was drunk, and Daisy hadn't long before had Jane. Faith found a way not to specifically acknowledge his offer. Later he told her he thought she was a lesbian. Having her know that just must've seemed like a good idea. A class act is The Roger.

The long, echoing dining hall has crisscrossed ceiling beams painted pink and light green and purple, a scheme apparently appropriate to Bavaria. There are long green-painted tables with pink and purple plastic folding chairs meant to promote an informal good time and family fun. Somewhere else in the lodge, Faith is certain, there is a better place to eat where you don't pay with coupons and nothing's pink or purple.

Faith is wearing a shiny Lycra bodysuit, over which she has put on her loden knickers and Norway socks. She looks superb, she believes. With anyone but Roger this would be fun, or at least a hoot.

Roger sits across the long table, too far away to talk easily. In a room that can conveniently hold five hundred souls, there are perhaps fifteen scattered diners. No one is eating family style, only solos and twos. Young lodge employees in paper caps wait dismally behind the long smorgasbord steam table. Metal heat lamps with orange beams are steadily overcooking the prime rib, of which

Roger has taken a goodly portion. Faith has chosen only a few green lettuce leaves, a beet round, two tiny ears of yellow corn, and no salad dressing. The sour smell of the Tyrol Room makes eating almost impossible.

"Do you know what I worry about?" Roger says, sawing around a triangle of glaucal gray roast beef fat, using a comically small knife. His tone implies he and Faith eat here together often and are just picking up where they've left off, as if they didn't hold each other in complete contempt.

"No," Faith says. "What?" Roger, she notices, has managed to hang on to his red smorgasbord coupon. The rule is you leave your coupon in the basket by the bread sticks. Clever Roger. Why, she wonders, is Roger tanned?

Roger smiles as though there's a lewd aspect to whatever it is that worries him. "I worry that Daisy's going to get so fixed up in rehab that she'll forget everything that's happened and want to be married again. To me, I mean. You know?" Roger chews as he talks. He wishes to seem earnest, his smile a serious, imploring, vacuous smile. This is Roger leveling. Roger owning up.

"That probably won't happen," Faith says. "I just have a feeling." She no longer wishes to look at her fragmentary salad. She does not have an eating disorder and could never have one.

"Maybe not." Roger nods. "I'd like to get out of guidance pretty soon, though. Start something new. Turn the page."

In truth, Roger is not bad-looking, only oppressively regular: small chin, small nose, small hands, small straight teeth—nothing unusual except his brown eyes are too narrow, as if he had Ukrainian blood. Daisy married him—she said—because of his alarmingly big dick. That—or more important, the lack of that—was in her view why many other marriages failed. When all else gave way, that would be there. Vince's, she'd shared, was even bigger. Ergo. It was to this particular quest that Daisy had dedicated her life. This, instead of college.

"What exactly would you like to do next?" Faith says. She is thinking how nice it would be if Daisy came out of rehab and *had* forgotten everything. A return to how things were when they still sort of worked often seemed a good solution.

"Well, it probably sounds crazy," Roger says, chewing, "but there's a company in Tennessee that takes apart jetliners for scrap. There's big money in it. I imagine it's how the movie business got started. Just some hare-brained scheme." Roger pokes at macaroni salad with his fork. A single Swedish meatball remains on his plate.

"It doesn't sound crazy," Faith lies, then looks longingly at the smorgasbord table. Maybe she's hungry, after all. But is the table full of food the smorgasbord, or is eating the food the smorgasbord?

Roger, she notices, has casually slipped his meal coupon into a pocket.

"Well, do you think you're going to do that?" Faith asks with reference to the genius plan of dismantling jet airplanes for big bucks.

"With the girls in school, it'd be hard," Roger admits soberly, ignoring what would seem to be obvious—that it is not a genius plan.

Faith gazes away again. She realizes no one else in the big room is dressed the way she is, which reminds her of who she is. She is not Snow Mountain Highlands (even if she once was). She is not Sandusky. She is not even Ohio. She is Hollywood. A fortress.

"I could take the girls for a while," she suddenly says. "I really wouldn't mind." She thinks of sweet Marjorie and sweet, unhappy Jane sitting on the Danish modern couch in their sweet nighties and monkey-face slippers, watching her trim the plastic rubber-tree plant. At the same moment, she thinks of Roger and Daisy being killed in an automobile crash on their triumphant way back from rehab. You can't help what you think.

"Where would they go to school?" Roger says, becoming alert to something unexpected. Something he might like.

"I'm sorry?" Faith says and flashes Roger, big-dick, narrow-eyed Roger a second movie star's smile. She has let herself become distracted by the thought of his timely death.

"I mean, like, where would they go to school?" Roger blinks. He is that alert.

"I don't know. Hollywood High, I guess. They have schools in California. I could find one."

"I'd have to think about it," Roger lies decisively.

"Okay, do," Faith says. Now that she has said this, without any previous thought of ever saying it, it becomes part of everyday reality. Soon she will become Jane and Marjorie's parent. Easy as that. "When you get settled in Tennessee you could have them back," she says without conviction.

"They probably wouldn't want to come back by then," Roger says. "Tennessee'd seem pretty dull."

"Ohio's dull. They like that."

"True," Roger says.

No one has thought to mention Daisy in promoting this new arrangement. Though Daisy, the mother, is committed elsewhere for the next little patch. And Roger needs to get his life jumpstarted, needs to put "guidance" in the rearview mirror. First things first.

The Pageant of Lights has gotten under way outside now— a ribbon of swaying torches gliding soundlessly down the expert slope like an overflow of human lava. All is preternaturally visible through the panoramic window. A large, bundled crowd of spectators has assembled at the bottom of the slope behind some snow fences, many holding candles in scraps of paper like at a Grateful Dead concert. All other artificial light is extinguished, except for the Yuletide spruce at the top. The young smorgasbord attendants, in their aprons and paper caps, have gathered at the window to witness the event yet again. Some are snickering. Someone remembers to turn the lights off in the Tyrol Room. Dinner is suspended.

"Do you downhill?" Roger asks, leaning over his empty plate in the half darkness. He is whispering, for some reason. Things could really turn out great, Faith understands him to be thinking: Eighty-six the girls. Dismantle plenty of jets. Just be friendly and it'll happen.

"No, never," Faith says, dreamily watching the torchbearers schussing side to side, a gradual, sinuous, dramaless tour downward. "It scares me."

"You'd get used to it." Roger unexpectedly reaches across the table to where her hands rest on either side of her uneaten salad. He touches, then pats, one of these hands. "And by the way," Roger says. "Thanks. I mean it. Thanks a lot."

BACK IN THE CONDO all is serene. Esther and the girls are still at the skating rink. Roger has wandered back to The Warming Shed. He has a girlfriend in Port Clinton, a former high-school counselee, now divorced. He will be calling her, telling her about his new Tennessee plans, adding that he wishes she were here at Snow Mountain Highlands with him and that his family could be in Rwanda. Bobbie, her name is.

A call to Jack is definitely in order. But first Faith decides to slide the newly trimmed rubber-tree plant nearer the window, where there's an outlet. When she plugs in, most of the white lights pop cheerily on. Only a few do not, and in the box are replacements. This is progress. Later, tomorrow, they can affix the star on top— her father's favorite ritual. "Now it's time for the star," he'd always say. "The star of the wise men." Her father had been a musician, a woodwind specialist. A man of talents, and of course a drunk. A specialist also in women who were not his wife. He had taught committedly at a junior college to make all their ends meet. He had wanted Faith to become a lawyer, so naturally she became one. Daisy he had no specific plans for, so naturally she became a drunk and sometime later, an energetic nymphomaniac. Eventually he died, at home. The paterfamilias. After that, but not until, her mother began to put weight on. "Well, there's my size, of course," was how she usually expressed it. She took it as a given: increase being the natural consequence of loss.

Whether to call Jack, though, in London or New York. (Nantucket is out, and Jack never keeps his cell phone on except for business hours.) Where is Jack? In London it was after midnight. In New York it was the same as here. Half past eight. And what message to leave? She could just say she was lonely; or that she had chest pains, or worrisome test results. (These would need to clear up mysteriously.)

But London, first. The flat in Sloane Terrace, half a block from the tube. They'd eaten breakfast at the Oriel, then Jack had gone off to work in The City while she did the Tate, the Bacons her specialty. So far from Snow Mountain Highlands—this being her sensation when dialing—a call going a great, great distance.

Ring-jing, ring-jing, ring-jing, ring-jing, ring-jing. Nothing.

There was a second number, for messages only, but she'd forgotten it. Call again to allow for a misdial. *Ring-jing, ring-jing, ring-jing . . .*

New York, then. East Fiftieth. Far, far east. The nice, small slice of river view. The bolt-hole he'd had since college. His freshman numerals framed. 1971. She'd gone to the trouble to have the bedroom redone. White everything. A smiling and tanned picture of herself from the boat, framed in red leather. Another of the two of them together at Cabo, on the beach. All similarly long distances from Snow Mountain Highlands.

Ring, ring, ring, ring. Then click. "Hi, this is Jack"— she almost says "Hi" back—"I'm not here right now, etc., etc., etc.," then a beep.

"Merry Christmas, it's me. Ummmm, Faith." She's stuck, but not at all flustered. She could just as well tell him everything. This happened today: the atomic energy smokestacks, the plastic rubber-tree plant, the Pageant of Lights, the smorgasbord, Eddie from years back, the girls' planned move to California. All things Christmas-y. "Ummm, I just wanted to say that I'm . . . fine, and that I trust— make that *hope*— that I *hope* you are too. I'll be back home— at the beach, that is— after Christmas. I'd love— make that like— to hear from you. I'm in Snow Mountain Highlands. In Michigan." She pauses, discussing with herself if there was further news worth relating. There isn't. Then she realizes (too late) she's treating his voice mail like her Dictaphone. There's no revising. Too bad. Her mistake. "Well, goodbye," she says, realizing this sounds a bit stiff, but doesn't revise. With them it's all over anyway. Who cares? She called.

OUT ON THE Nordic Trail 1, lights, soft white ones not unlike the Christmas tree lights in the condo, have been strung in selected fir boughs—bright enough that you'd never get lost in the dark, dim enough not to spoil the mysterious effect.

She does not actually enjoy this kind of skiing either. Not really. Not with all the tiresome waxing, the stiff rental shoes, the long inconvenient skis, the sweaty underneath, the chance that all this could eventuate in catching cold and missing work. The gym is better. Major heat, then quick you're clean and back in the car, back in the office. Back on the phone. She is a sport, but definitely not a sports nut. Still, this is not terrifying.

No one accompanies her on nighttime Nordic Trail 1, the Pageant of the Lights having lured away the other skiers. Two Japanese were conversing at the trail head, small beige men in bright chartreuse Lycras—smooth, serious faces, giant thighs, blunt, no-nonsense arms—commencing the rigorous course, "The Beast," Nordic Trail 3. On their rounded, stocking-capped heads they'd worn tiny lights like coal miners to light their way. They have disappeared immediately.

Here the snow virtually hums to the sound of her sliding strokes. A full moon rides behind filigree clouds as she strides forward in the near darkness of crusted woods. There is wind she can hear high up in the tallest pines and hemlocks, but at ground level there's none, just cold radiating off the metallic snow. Only her ears actually feel cold, that and the sweat line of her hair. Her heartbeat barely registers. She is in shape.

For an instant she hears distant music, a singing voice with orchestral accompaniment. She pauses to listen. The music's pulse travels through the trees. Strange. Possibly it's Roger, she thinks, between deep breaths; Roger onstage in the karaoke bar, singing his greatest hits to other lonelies in the dark. "Blue Bayou," "Layla," "Tommy," "Try to Remember." Roger at a safe distance. Her hair, she realizes, is shining in the moonlight. If she were being watched, she would at least look good.

But wouldn't it be romantic to peer down from these woods through the dark and spy some shining, many-winged lodge flying below, windows ablaze, like an exotic casino from some Paul Muni movie. Graceful skaters adrift on a lighted rink. A garlanded lift still in stately motion, a few, last alpinists taking their silken, torchless float before lights-out. The great tree shining from the summit.

Except, this is not a particularly pretty part of Michigan. Nothing's to see—dark trunks, cold dead falls, swags of heavy snow hung in the spruce boughs.

And she is stiffening. Just that fast. New muscles being visited. Best not to go so far.

Daisy, her sister, comes to mind. Daisy, who will soon exit the hospital with a whole new view of life. Inside, there's of course been the twelve-step ritual to accompany the normal curriculum of deprivation and regret. And someone, somewhere, at some time possibly even decades back, will definitely turn out to have touched Daisy in ways inappropriate and detrimental to her well-being, and at an all-too-tender age. And not just once, but many times, over a series of terrible, silent years. The culprit possibly an older, suspicious neighborhood youth—a loner—or a far too avuncular school librarian. Even the paterfamilias will come under posthumous scrutiny (the historical perspective, as always, unprovable and therefore indisputable).

And certain sacrifices of dignity will naturally be requested of everyone then, due to this rich new news from the past: a world so much more lethal than anyone believed, nothing being the way we thought it was; so much hidden from view; if anyone had only known, could've spoken out and opened up the lines of communication, could've trusted, confided, blah, blah, blah. Their mother will, necessarily, have suspected nothing, but unquestionably should've. Perhaps Daisy, herself, will have suggested that Faith is a lesbian. The snowball effect. No one safe, no one innocent.

Up ahead, in the shadows, a mile into the trek, Shelter 1 sits to the right of Nordic Trail 1—a darkened clump in a small clearing, a place to rest and wait for the others to catch up (if there were others). A perfect place to turn back.

Shelter 1 is nothing fancy, a simple rustic school-bus enclosure open on one side and hewn from logs. Out on the snow lie crusts of dinner rolls, a wedge of pizza, some wadded tissues, three beer cans—treats for the forest creatures—each casting its tiny shadow upon the white surface.

Although seated in the gloomy inside on a plank bench are not school kids, but Roger, the brother-in-law, in his powder-blue ski suit and hiking boots. He is not singing karaoke after all. She noticed no boot tracks up the trail. Roger is more resourceful than at first he seems.

"It's eff-ing cold up here." Roger speaks from within the shadows of Shelter 1. He is not wearing his black glasses now, and is barely visible, though she senses he's smiling—his brown eyes even narrower.

"What are you doing up here, Roger?" Faith asks.

"Oh," Roger says out of the gloom. "I just thought I'd come up." He crosses his arms and extends his hiking boots into the snow light like some species of high-school toughie.

"What for?" Her knees are both knotted and weak from exertion. Her heart has begun thumping. Perspiration is cold on her lip. Temperatures are in the low twenties. In winter the most innocent places turn lethal.

"Nothing ventured," Roger says. He is mocking her.

"This is where I'm turning around," Faith ventures. "Would you like to go back down the hill with me?" What she wishes for is more light. Much more light. A bulb in the shelter would be very good. Bad things happen in the dark that would prove unthinkable in the light.

"Life leads you to some pretty interesting places, doesn't it, Faith?"

She would like to smile and not feel menaced by Roger, who should be with his daughters.

"I guess," she says. She can smell alcohol in the dry air. He is drunk and is winging all of this. A bad occurrence.

"You're very pretty. *Very* pretty. The big lawyer," Roger says. "Why don't you come in here?"

"Oh, no thank you," Faith says. Roger is loathsome, but he is also family, and she feels paralyzed by not knowing what to do— a most unusual situation. She wishes to be more agile on her skis, to leap upward and discover herself turned around and already gliding away.

"I always thought that in the right situation, we could have some big-time fun," Roger goes on.

"Roger, this isn't a good thing to be doing," whatever he's doing. She wants to glare at him, then understands her knees are quivering. She feels very, very tall on her skis, unusually accessible.

"It *is* a good thing to be doing," Roger says. "It's what I came up here for. Some fun."

"I don't want us to do anything up here, Roger," Faith says. "Is that all right?" This, she realizes, is what fear feels like— the way you'd feel in a late-night parking structure, or jogging alone in an isolated factory area, or entering your house in the wee hours, fumbling for your key. Accessible. And then, suddenly, there would be someone. Bingo. A man with oppressively ordinary looks who lacks a plan.

"Nope, nope. That's absolutely not all right." Roger stands up but stays in the sheltered darkness. "The lawyer," he says again, still grinning.

"I'm just going to turn around," Faith says, and very unsteadily begins to move her long left ski up out of its track, and then, leaning on her poles, her right ski up and out of its track. It is dizzying, and her calves ache, and it is complicated not to cross her ski tips. But it is essential to remain standing. To fall would mean surrender. What is the skiing expression? Tele . . . tele-something. She wishes she could tele-something. Tele-something the hell away from here. Her thighs burn. In California, she thinks, she is an officer of the court. A public official, sworn to uphold the law—though not to enforce it. She is a force for good.

"You look stupid standing there," Roger says stupidly.

She intends to say nothing more. There is nothing really to say. Talk is not cheap now, and she is concentrating very hard. For a moment she thinks she hears music again, music far away. It can't be.

"When you get all the way around," Roger says, "then I want to show you something." He does not say what. In her mind—moving her skis inches at a time, her ankles heavy—in her mind she says, "Then what?" but doesn't say that.

"I really hate your eff-ing family," Roger says. His boots go crunch on the snow. She glances over her shoulder, but to look at him is too much. He is approaching. She will fall and then dramatic, regrettable things will happen. In a gesture he possibly deems dramatic, Roger—though she cannot see it—unzips his blue snowsuit front. He intends her to hear this noise. She is three-quarters turned around. She could see him over her left shoulder if she chose to. Have a look, see what all the excitement's about. She is sweating. Underneath she is drenched.

"Yep, life leads you to some pretty interesting situations." He is repeating himself. There is another zipping noise. This is big-time in Roger's worldview.

"Yes," she says, "it does." She has come almost fully around now.

She hears Roger laugh a little chuckle, an unhumorous "hunh." Then he says, "Almost." She hears his boots squeeze. She feels his actual self close beside her. This undoubtedly will help to underscore how much he hates her family.

Then there are voices—saving voices—behind her. She cannot help looking over her left shoulder now and up the trail where it climbs into the dark trees. There is a light, followed by another light, like stars coming down from on high. Voices, words, language she doesn't quite understand. Japanese. She does not look at Roger, but simply slides one ski, her left one, forward into its track, lets her right one follow and find its way, pushes on her poles. And in just that small allotment of time and with that amount of effort she is away. She thinks she hears Roger say something, another "hunh," a kind of grunting sound, but she can't be sure.

IN THE CONDO everyone is sleeping. The plastic rubber-tree lights are twinkling. They reflect from the window that faces the ski hill, which now is dark. Someone, Faith notices (her mother), has devoted much time to replacing the spent bulbs so the tree can fully twinkle. The gold star, the star that led the wise men, is lying on the coffee table like a starfish, waiting to be properly affixed.

Marjorie, the younger, sweeter sister, is asleep on the orange couch, under the Brueghel scene. She has left her bed to sleep near the tree, brought her quilted pink coverlet with her.

Naturally Faith has locked Roger out. Roger can die alone and cold in the snow. Or he can sleep in a doorway or by a steam pipe somewhere in the Snow Mountain Highlands complex and explain his situation to the security staff. Roger will not sleep with his pretty daughters this night. She is taking a hand in things now. These girls are hers. Though, how naïve of her not to know that an offer to take the girls would immediately be translated by Roger into an invitation to fuck him. She has been in California too long, has fallen out of touch with things middle American. How strange that Roger, too, would say *eff-ing*. He probably also says *X-mas*.

At the ice rink, two teams are playing hockey under high white lights. A red team opposes a black team. Net cages have been brought on, the larger rink walled down to regulation size and shape. A few spectators stand watching—wives and girlfriends. Boyne City versus Petoskey; Cadillac versus Sheboygan, or some such. The little girls' own white skates are piled by the door she has now safely locked with a dead bolt.

It would be good to put the star on, she thinks. "Now it's time for the star." Who knows what tomorrow will bring? The arrival of wise men couldn't hurt.

So, with the flimsy star, which is made of slick aluminum paper and is large and gold and weightless and five-pointed, Faith stands on the Danish dining-table chair and fits the slotted fastener onto the topmost leaf of the rubber-tree plant. It is not a perfect fit by any means, there being no spring at the pinnacle, so that the star doesn't stand up as much as it leans off the top in a sad, comic, but also victorious way. (This use was never envisioned by the Filipino tree makers.) Tomorrow others can all add to the tree, invent ornaments from absurd or inspirational raw materials. Tomorrow Roger himself will be rehabilitated and become everyone's best friend. Except hers.

Marjorie's eyes have opened, though she has not stirred on the couch. For a moment, but only for a moment, she appears dead. "I went to sleep," she says softly and blinks her brown eyes.

"Oh, I saw you," Faith smiles. "I thought you were another Christmas present. I thought Santa had been here early and left you for me." She takes a careful seat on the spindly coffee table, close beside Marjorie—in case there would be some worry to express, a gloomy dream to relate. A fear. She smooths her hand through Marjorie's warm hair.

Marjorie takes a deep breath and lets air go out smoothly through her nostrils. "Jane's asleep," she says.

"And how would you like to go back to bed?" Faith whispers. Possibly she hears a soft tap on the door—the door she has dead-bolted. The door she will not open. The door beyond which the world and trouble wait. Marjorie's eyes wander toward the sound, then swim again with sleep. She is safe.

"Leave the tree on," Marjorie instructs, though asleep.

"Sure, okay, sure," Faith says. "The tree stays. We keep the tree."

She eases her hand under Marjorie, who, by old habit, reaches, caresses her neck. In an instant she has Marjorie in her arms, pink coverlet and all, carrying her altogether effortlessly into the darkened bedroom where her sister sleeps on one of the twin beds. Carefully she lowers Marjorie onto the empty bed and re-covers her. Again she thinks she hears soft tapping, though it stops. She believes it will not come again this night.

Jane is sleeping with her face to the wall, her breathing deep and audible. Jane is the good sleeper, Marjorie the less reliable one. Faith stands in the middle of the dark, windowless room, between the twin beds, the blinking Christmas lights haunting the stillness that has come at such expense. The room smells musty and dank, as if it's been closed for months and opened just for this purpose, this night, these children. If only briefly she is reminded of Christmases she might've once called her own. "Okay," she whispers. "Okay, okay, okay."

FAITH UNDRESSES IN the master suite, too tired to shower. Her mother sleeps on one side of their shared bed. She is a small mountain, visibly breathing beneath the covers. A glass of red wine, half drunk, sits on the bed table beside her molded neck brace. A picture of a white sailboat on a calm blue ocean hangs over the bed. Faith half closes the door to undress, the blinking Christmas lights shielded.

She will wear pajamas tonight, for her mother's sake. She has bought a new pair. White, pure silk, smooth as water. Blue silk piping.

And here is the unexpected sight of herself in the cheap, wavy door mirror. All good. Just the same pale scar where a cyst was notched from her left breast, a meaningless scar no one would see. But a good effect still. Thin, hard thighs. A small nice belly. Boy's hips. The whole package, nothing to complain about.

There's need of a glass of water. Always take a glass of water to bed, never a glass of red wine. When she passes by the living-room window, her destination the tiny kitchen, she sees that the hockey game is now over. It is after midnight. The players are shaking hands on the ice, others are skating in wide circles. On the expert slope above the rink, lights have been turned on again. Machines with headlights groom the snow at treacherous angles and great risk.

And she sees Roger. He is halfway between the ice rink and the condos, walking back in his powder-blue suit. He has watched the hockey game, no doubt. Roger stops and looks up at her where she stands in the window in her white pj's, the Christmas tree lights blinking as her background. He stops and stares. He has found his black-frame glasses. His mouth is moving, but he makes no gesture. There is no room at this inn for Roger.

In bed, her mother is even larger. A great heat source, vaguely damp when Faith touches her back. Her mother is wearing blue gingham, a nightdress not so different from the muumuu she wears in daylight. She smells unexpectedly good. Rich.

How long, Faith wonders, has it been since she's slept with her mother. A hundred years? Twenty? But good that it would seem so normal.

She has left the door open in case the girls should call, in case they wake up and are afraid, in case they miss their father. The Christmas lights blink off and on merrily beyond the doorway. She can hear snow slide off the roof, an automobile with chains jingling softly somewhere out of sight. She has intended to call for messages but let it slip.

And how long ago, she wonders, was her mother slim and pretty? The sixties? Not so long ago, really. She had been a girl then. They—the sixties—always seem so close. Though to her mother probably not.

Blink, blink, blink, the lights blink.

Marriage. Yes, naturally she would think of that now. Though maybe marriage was only a long plain of self-revelation at the end of which there's someone else who doesn't know you very well. That would be a message she could've left for Jack. "Dear Jack, I now know that marriage is a long plain at the end of which there's etc., etc., etc." You always thought of these things too late. Somewhere, Faith hears more faint music, "Away in a Manger," played prettily on chimes. It is music to sleep to.

And how would they deal with tomorrow? Not the eternal tomorrow, but the promised, practical one. Her thighs feel stiff, yet she is slowly relaxing. Her mother, the mountain beside her, is facing away. How indeed? Roger would be rehabilitated tomorrow, yes, yes. There will be board games. Changes of outfits. Phone calls placed. She will find the time to ask her mother if anyone had ever been abused, and find out, happily, not. Unusual looks will be passed between and among everyone. Certain names, words will be in short supply, for the sake of all. The girls will again learn to ski and to enjoy it. Jokes will be told. They will feel better, be a family again. Christmas takes care of its own.

A Christmas Pageant

by Donna Tartt

The lunchroom, even with all its tinsel and lights and cutouts of Santa Claus, still looked like the lunchroom: concrete floor, windowless cinder-block walls, long humming lights that were encased in things like egg cartons across the ceiling and were different from the lights Sally had at home. She remembered sitting under those same lights in the first grade, hungry but not wanting to eat her chicken sandwich because Leah had made it, because it was something from home, and the thrumming, green-ish light had made her want to cry. Now she was in the fourth grade, but the lights still made her feel homesick and sad. She had never been in the lunchroom at night before. Even at night it was exactly the same, and made her feel the same way.

Tonight the tables were folded up and the chairs were arranged in rows. A wooden platform that looked homemade stood against the back wall. Mrs. Mills's fourth-grade class was having its Christmas pageant.

Everybody was dressed up, and some of the little girls looked as though they had been at the beauty parlor, but Sally's hair was short and she hadn't gone. She was wearing a plaid pinafore, a white shirt and red leotard, and black patent-leather shoes. Usually she liked this outfit but tonight she had not wanted to wear it because it seemed irreverent. In her room, before leaving home, she had searched about hastily for something that would make her look more religious; at last, she draped a white dresser-scarf over her head. It made her look like a bride, or the Virgin Mary. For a while she practiced supplicant poses in the mirror—holding her hands out, palms up, eyes turned to heaven. Then Leah, the maid, had come in without Sally seeing her and laughed. It irritated Sally, but still she wanted very badly to wear the dresser-scarf; she had lied to Leah, telling her that everybody was supposed to wear them, and had gotten a swat on the hand.

Sally's part was the letter T in the word *Christmas.* Each child was to wear a big sign with the proper letter, and they were to step forward and explain what their letter meant when the time came. The C in Christmas stood for candy, the H for holly, and so forth. Sally's part went like this:

> T is for tinsel
> Bright as the dawning
> Which makes us so happy
> On Christmas morning.

It was a silly poem, not a real one. Mrs. Mills had made it up. Besides which, the letters did not stand for what Mrs. Mills said they did. C stood for Christ, not candy; H was certainly for Herod. Sally had wanted to be M because that stood for Mary, but she was glad that Mrs. Mills had picked Kenny Priddy and not her because Mrs. Mills had made it mean mistletoe, and that meant kissing, and people would laugh.

Sally had tried to explain this to her best friend, a little girl named Tammy Dankin. Tammy was not popular and sometimes her nose ran, but Sally liked her because she would play the games that Sally liked to play, games that were generally religious in nature and that usually involved Sally falling on the ground and pretending to be dead while Tammy knelt at her side and implored God to revive her. Sally had a gift for remaining completely motionless in these postures, hardly breathing even when Tammy shook her or pulled her hair; sometimes she would lie so still that Tammy would become frightened and begin to cry.

Tammy was sitting with another girl, a little fat girl, across the room; both of them had reindeer horns tied to their heads and they were sharing mixed nuts from a paper cup. Sally saw Tammy looking over at her wistfully and she turned her head away very slowly, so Tammy would know it was on purpose and that she was still not speaking to her.

A few weeks before, at recess, Sally had drawn Tammy aside from a game of jump rope especially to explain how Mrs. Mills had left all mention of Christ out of the Christmas pageant, and why the Christmas pageant was sacrilege, and how they must both take up the burden of prayer and penance in order to appease God's wrath against Mrs. Mills. "It shall be better for her," Sally had explained, "if she had had a millstone around her neck and were thrown into the sea." But Tammy was impatient; she kept glancing around and bumping her knees together; at last, she had said, "I *like* Mrs. Mills," and had run back to her game.

Before, Sally had asked God for mercy; now she prayed to Him for vengeance. She felt that her prayer would be answered, as her penance had been quite severe. She had walked around the house blindfolded until Leah heard her bumping into things and made her take the blindfold off; she had brought the scratchy wire door-mat up to her bedroom from the toolshed so that she could kneel on it at night to pray; for the last week she had thrown away her sandwich at lunchtime and refused her dessert at night. She had prayed for the most spectacular things she could think of, all the very worst things in the Bible she could find: for rains of fire, for locusts, for the profaned lunchroom to tumble down around her ears like the temple had fallen around Samson. Now, with the pageant starting soon, she rested in the knowledge that God would deliver her.

Suddenly Sally felt a large hand dig into her upper arm; she turned and saw Mrs. Mills towering over her, her big silly eyes popping like Bing cherries. She had on the Christmas corsage the class had given her and she was wearing a red knit dress with a tie at the waist that made her stomach pooch out even more than it usually did. Her brittle, peach-colored hair was piled high on her head but already the curls looked rubbed and worn, like doll hair; Sally thought, with some satisfaction, about the time she had heard her mother say that Mrs. Mills ought not to go around with such messy hair. "Poor old thing," her mother had said. "Maybe she can't afford to have it fixed."

"Sally," said Mrs. Mills severely. She did not let go of Sally's arm, which made Sally mad; she did not like it when Mrs. Mills touched her. "I don't know what you think you're doing over here. You ought to be over there with the Christmas letters. You don't even have on your costume yet."

"Yes, ma'am," Sally said quickly and tried to pull away.

"Now scat," Mrs. Mills said, and gave Sally a swat on the behind with the copy of the program she was holding.

There shall be weeping, thought Sally, face burning, *and wailing, and gnashing of teeth.*

THE CHRISTMAS LETTERS were all standing in a straggly line by the lunchroom door, waiting to have their costumes fixed and drinking cups of punch. A couple of mothers were helping with the costumes, and Sally was unhappy to see that Tammy's mother, Mrs. Dankin, was among them. Toward the beginning of school, Sally had been in the grocery store with Leah, and Mrs. Dankin, pushing a shopping cart, had come up to speak to them. After asking Sally a question or two about school, she had turned to Leah. "This one," she said, nodding at Sally, "has quite an imagination."

"Ma'am?" said Leah.

"You really wouldn't believe," said Mrs. Dankin, in a bright voice, but with a mean sideways look at Sally, "some of the crazy stuff she's been telling Tammy." It had looked for a moment as if she would elaborate, and Sally had thought she might cry, but Leah, unexpectedly, had been very sweet. "This baby is mighty smart," she said sharply to Mrs. Dankin. "She knew how to read when she was three." Still, it had all been very embarrassing. She was glad her mother hadn't been there; then again, her mother had Leah and never had to go to the grocery store like Mrs. Dankin did.

Mrs. Dankin, together with somebody else's mother, was fixing Frankie Detweiler's costume. He was to be the letter I, for icicle; the mothers were absentmindedly draping Christmas-tree icicles over his shoulders and talking. Sally, keeping her eyes straight ahead, listened to their conversation. It was very interesting. Mrs. Dankin was telling the other mother that very early the morning before, she had woken up to someone beating on the glass pane of the back door of her kitchen. *"Beating,"* said Mrs. Dankin, "just slapping up against it with both hands, over and over." She let the icicles she was holding fall on Frankie's shoulder and held up both palms to demonstrate.

"That's awful," said the other mother, fascinated.

"Well, do you know who it was? It was that awful Henry Lee Priddy." (*Was that Kenny's father?* wondered Sally.) "And he just kept beating on the glass and yelling, 'I'm drunk, I'm drunk, call the *po*lice, I'm drunk.'"

"Did you wake up Ray?" said the other mother.

"I sure did," said Mrs. Dankin grimly.

The voices sank to a whisper.

Sally thought about this. Why had this been such a bad thing, when Mr. Priddy had only wanted to turn himself in? She was still wondering about this after they had stopped whispering and resumed normal conversation, which was very boring and about people she didn't know. Then, with a horrible start, she heard her own mother's name: *Christine Farquhar.*

". . . not surprised she's not here."

"I don't know what Christine does with her time."

"I don't either. She's got a maid, and a cook, and she doesn't have a job, and she just gives that little girl to the niggers to raise."

Little girl, thought Sally, her face reddening. So now they were talking about her. And they had called Leah *nigger.* Anybody knew that wasn't nice.

"Maybe it's the niggers tell her all that nutty stuff about hell. I can't figure where else she gets it. It scares poor Tammy. The other night she woke up crying. Ray had to go in and talk to her."

"I wonder why she's like that," said the other mother. "Christine doesn't seem very religious."

My mother is prettier than you, Sally wanted to say to them, *lots prettier, she has more money and her hair is really red, not dyed like yours is.* They would be sorry for this. She would go home and tell Leah and Leah's husband would go out and shoot them. Leah's husband was named Jackson. He had been in jail before.

Sally was thinking about Jackson, about how Mrs. Dankin would look if she opened the back door of her kitchen and saw Jackson standing there with a gun, when she felt a sharp jab from a fingernail in her left arm. She turned, irritably, and saw Kenny Priddy, who was the letter M, holding up two crossed fingers.

"Sally germs, vaccinated," he said, in a twangy, leering singsong; with a shiver she noticed how dirty and long his fingernails were. For a moment she thought of telling him that he wasn't playing the game right, that what did she care if she got a dose of her own germs; instead, she turned away.

"Is your mama here?" said Kenny, leaning over. Sally did not answer. "Hey, I'm talking to you," he said, grabbing her by the arm. "Is your mama here or what?"

Sally looked at him, at his eager, rattish face, at his dirty hair and clothes. He was trembling all over with excitement like a Chihuahua. You were supposed to feel sorry for people like Kenny because he lived in a trailer and was poor. Sally did not see how anyone could feel sorry for Kenny, though, even Jesus. He was mean to animals and had failed a grade. "No," she said.

"That's 'cause your mama don't love you," said Kenny, looking satisfied. "Your mama is a big fat snotwad."

"My mother is not here," said Sally, "because she is in the hospital having her appendix removed." This was a lie. Sally's mother was actually at a party out at the country club.

"My mama's here," said Kenny, and pointed to a woman in the sixth or seventh row. The woman had Kenny's close-set eyes; her hair was gray-blond like his, too, and all dirty and limp. Unlike the other mothers, who were all dressed up, she had on blue jeans with a hole at the knee and a T-shirt from a motorcycle dealership. Under the T-shirt her chest was all caved in, flat as a man's. Nobody was talking to her, not even the other tacky-looking mothers, and she had her arms folded over the purse in her lap as if she thought somebody would want to steal it. Then the purse moved; Sally, startled, saw that it was not a purse at all, but a baby.

"Ain't she pretty," said Kenny. He meant it, too, and that was sad. "Them's my brothers next to her, Darryl and Wayne. That baby in her lap's only my stepsister. Her name's Misty Darlene."

He went on talking about the new baby but Sally wasn't paying attention. Mrs. Dankin and the other mother were putting the final touches on S for snow's costume. Next in line was Sally.

"I almost didn't have to be in this stupid play," said Kenny conversationally. "My daddy came to town to get me for the weekend but they're not suppose to let me see him. He lives at French Camp. I got a brother down at the reform school at French Camp. My daddy," he said proudly, "just got out of prison."

"*Really,*" said Sally, turning around to look at Kenny. Saint Paul had been in prison. "What did he do?"

Kenny shifted to the other foot. "Something about statutory," he said.

"That's very interesting," said Sally. She was about to ask what that was when suddenly there were Mrs. Dankin and the other mother, leaning over her. "You're T for tinsel," said Mrs. Dankin, as if Sally didn't know what her own part was. Meekly Sally bent her head, like a pony waiting for the bridle, and allowed the sign that said T to be put around her neck.

"Know why you have to be T?" crowed Kenny. He was hopping from foot to foot and trembling with joy. "Because you smell just like tee-tee, that's—"

"Hush up," said Mrs. Dankin to him nastily. "You'll be wearing one of these yourself in a minute." Mrs. Dankin didn't like Kenny any more than Sally did.

The other mother, her arms draped with tinsel, walked around Sally and looked at her in a dissatisfied fashion, lifting up a piece of Sally's hair—dark, bobbed at the nape like a Chinaman's. "I don't know why a child with long hair wasn't chosen for this part," she said. "We could have braided the tinsel in it if it was just a little longer."

"Sally, what'd you want to get your hair cut short for?" said Mrs. Dankin pleasantly.

Sally's face felt very hot. "My mother won't let me have long hair until I'm old enough to take care of it myself," she said. "My mother says long hair on little girls is tacky."

Mrs. Dankin exchanged a disgusted look with the other mother, and suddenly Sally remembered: Tammy Dankin had hair halfway down her back. But it was true: her mother really did say that. Besides, having short hair meant that you Denied the World.

Mrs. Dankin cleared her throat and picked up a string of gold tinsel. "Will your mother be here tonight?" she said as she wound it in a circle around Sally's head.

The tinsel prickled her forehead. "No, ma'am," she said.

Mrs. Dankin raised her penciled eyebrows as though she were really surprised. "Oh, no? That's a shame. Why not?"

"She is out of town," said Sally. All of a sudden she felt like she might cry.

"That's not really festive enough, do you think, Carol?" said the other mother, stepping out from behind Sally's back and looking concerned. "Just that little piece on her head makes her look like she's supposed to be an angel."

They were quiet a moment, looking at her. All of a sudden Kenny began to jump up and down. "I want my costume, I want my costume," he sang in a high, breathless voice.

Mrs. Dankin turned on him. "Do you know how to stand still?" she snapped.

"I'VE GOT SOME mistletoe," sang Kenny to Sally, holding a sprig of mistletoe that he'd torn off his costume up over her head and sticking his face in hers. "I guess that means we should kiss." There was a big red smear across his mouth from the Christmas punch. Sally turned her head away.

The Christmas letters, shuffling, restless, were waiting in the hall outside the lunchroom, being watched by a couple of mothers. They were to go on after Santa's elves. She could hear them in the lunchroom now, singing their stupid song. Mrs. Mills was making some mistakes on the piano. She couldn't play very well.

Kenny nudged Sally in the ribs with his elbow. "If I wanted to," he said, "I could beat you up. Right here."

Sally paid no attention to him. Her stomach hurt and the lights were too bright; "Jingle Bell Rock" had given way to the elves and "I Saw Mommy Kissing Santa Claus"; already the birth of Christ had been sadly profaned, yet somehow God allowed the pageant to go on.

"What you looking over there at the pay phone for?" Kenny said to her. "You think your boyfriend's gonna call you or something?"

God will put out the lamps of the wicked; He will banish the unclean.

"Who's your boyfriend?" said Kenny, leaning closer. "I bet he's retarded."

With a sinking feeling, Sally heard Mrs. Mills bang out the final notes on the piano. The mothers, inside the lunchroom, began to clap.

"I know a retarded boy," said Kenny pleasantly. "His name is Tom Bibbett. What he does, is, go around all the time with a straight pin and pretend to give everyone shots. He's my first cousin, I guess."

"Hush," said a mother who was coming along the rear of the line. "Single file, everybody."

Kenny waited until she had passed and then resumed. "Every day Tom Bibbett has to take the bus into Tupelo to the Mental Retardation. He knows a lot of other retarded kids. Probably he knows your boyfriend."

The mother, now at the head of the line, turned. "Who's that still talking back there?"

"Kenny," said Rosemary Mitchell and Frankie Detweiler at the same time, in tired voices.

"Well, you tell him to hush up." She opened the door to the lunchroom; a flag of light fell into the hall. "Go on," she whispered to the C, and gave him a little push.

SALLY COULDN'T SEE anything, just a few stout, beaming faces in the first row; the sound of applause rolled over her. Flashbulbs popped here and there. Somebody had a movie camera and was walking backward with it down the aisle, all crouched over. Then the clapping died down and there was no sound at all except the rustling of programs and the whir of the movie camera.

"C is for candy,"

said the C hesitantly; he was in the slow reading circle:

"Chocolate and mints
That we get in our stockings
After lots of . . ."

"Small hints," said a voice somewhere near the stage.

"Small hints," repeated the C, gratefully.

Without waiting for the C's applause to stop, the H rushed into her poem, saying the words really fast so everyone would know how well she knew them by heart:

"H is for holly
All red and green
It's the prettiest thing
That I've ever seen."

Next was Tammy Dankin. She had her head to the side and was making her eyes big on purpose:

"R is for reindeer,"

she said, in a high, babyish voice; did she think people didn't know she was putting it on?

"Stomping their hoofs
And bringing us presents
When they land on our roofs."

"Awww," said the mothers when she had finished, and clapped very loudly. They had been taken in by the baby voice and by Tammy's size; she was the littlest girl in the class. Tammy giggled and, to Sally's disgust, curtsied. Tammy was like one of those bad children of Israel in captivity; she knew better and yet was happy to do wrong and show off if anyone at all approved.

It was all going so fast, much faster than Sally had expected; somehow she had thought it would take hours. In a few moments it would be her turn. Her eyes were filling with tears; she couldn't see anything but a fuzz of brightness.

"I is for icicle,"

whined Frankie Detweiler; he was trying hard to be cute, too:

"So frosty and white
Which hangs from the roof
On a long winter's—"

All of a sudden the door to the lunchroom flew open and slammed against the wall with a crash.

Sally jerked her head up; the mothers, startled, all craned to look. Mrs. Mills got up from her place at the piano and flustered over to the door.

The mothers all began to whisper.

"Hey," said Frankie.

They could hear Mrs. Mills by the door now, squeaking, breathless. "I'm sorry, sir, but we're in the middle of our little program right now. Why don't you just come in and—"

"Outta my way."

Mrs. Mills pattered backward, her big loony eyes rolling, and the hum of whispers from the mothers stopped.

It was a man, in a greasy T-shirt, cowboy boots, and jeans. He was huge, red-eyed, unshaven; blue and black tattoos snaked luridly up his forearms; there was a bottle of whiskey in his hand. He staggered out to the front of the stage and stood there for a moment, blinded by the spotlight, one arm thrown up to shade his eyes, blinking, reeling. "RaeLynn," he said hoarsely. "Where are you, RaeLynn Priddy?"

"Hey," said Kenny, interested. "That's my *dad.*"

There was the quick sound of a chair being scraped back, and Kenny's mother jumped up. "Get out of here before I call the cops, Henry Lee," she yelled at him. "You ain't got no—"

Mr. Priddy lurched forward; his foot caught in the cord to the Christmas lights and he almost fell. With a savage kick he sent the cord flying out of the socket, and half the room went black. Someone screamed. "I come for my kid," he said.

"Over my dead body," yelled Kenny's mother.

"Maybe," said the man.

There was a click and a glint in the spotlight; someone else screamed, and then someone else. Mr. Priddy had a big deer knife in his hand.

"Mr. Yopp!" shrieked Mrs. Mills. "Somebody run find Mr.

Yopp!" Mr. Yopp was a retired electrician; he was the janitor at the elementary school.

Mr. Priddy came toward Kenny's mother with the knife, walking very carefully, one foot placed cautiously in front of the other. The mothers in the front rows began to scatter.

Kenny's mother was holding Misty Darlene in front of her, like a shield. "Get that goddamn knife away from me."

Mr. Priddy, with a jerk of the knife, motioned toward the stage and licked his lips. "Go on up there and get him," he said.

"Get him yourself," said Kenny's mother, holding Misty Darlene defensively in front of her face.

Mr. Priddy made a quick feint toward the side of her face with the knife. "*You* better go get him," he said, "if you don't want me to slit your nose wide open with this here knife."

Kenny's mother lowered the baby and stared at him contemptuously. "You ain't gonna do shit," she said.

There was a quick flash of silver; the next second, Kenny's mother was standing very still, and her eyes were wide, and Mr. Priddy had his arm around her neck and the knife at the end of her tiny, pinched nose. "Hell, RaeLynn," he said in her ear, in an aw-shucks kind of voice, full of regret. "You know I will."

Mrs. Mills was still crying for Mr. Yopp. Sally wondered what she thought Mr. Yopp would be able to do even if he had been there. Mr. Yopp was about seventy years old; he had lost an arm in an accident down at the power plant.

Mr. Priddy was behind Kenny's mother now, his elbow still around her neck and the knife at her nose. Roughly, with his knee in the back of her legs, he was making her walk down the aisle toward the stage, Misty Darlene still in her arms, blinking, somber.

"The kids!" somebody screamed.

"Run," screamed somebody else, but most of the kids had already scattered. Only Kenny remained on the stage, and Sally, and Tammy Dankin, who was crying and too scared to run.

"Tammy!" screamed Mrs. Dankin. She was kneeling on the floor to the left of the stage, her arms outstretched. "Run here! Run to Mama!"

Mr. Priddy was walking up the steps of the stage with Mrs. Priddy in front of him; as he got her up on the platform and was edging her across it, he bumped against Tammy—weeping, the reindeer horns now slipped from place and poking out from the side of her head—and made her stumble. Mrs. Dankin screeched and rushed onto the platform, almost knocking both Mr. and Mrs. Priddy over (more horrified screams from the audience, as for a moment it looked as if Mrs. Priddy were not only going to drop the baby but lose her nose); the whiskey bottle slipped from Mr. Priddy's free hand and broke on the floor.

"Sorry, Rae," said Mr. Priddy breathlessly and pulled himself up. "What the hell, lady," he snapped, and then he stopped and looked at Mrs. Dankin more closely.

Mrs. Dankin, her eyes glassy and her arm around the sobbing Tammy, began slowly to back away.

"Just a minute," said Mr. Priddy, narrowing his eyes at Mrs. Dankin, who was still inching backward. "I said just a minute," he snarled, catching Mrs. Priddy in a half nelson with his free arm and swinging the arm with the knife around, and Mrs. Dankin stopped, the tears drying on her cheeks and her eyes round with terror.

"Oh, no!" screamed somebody in the audience. "He's going to kill them!"

"*You,*" said Mr. Priddy to Mrs. Dankin, between his teeth, "are the bitch who sicced that dog on me the other night."

Mrs. Dankin, stuttering, tried to say something or other that didn't come out right at all.

"That damn dog like to chewed my leg off. Get the boy, Rae-Lynn," he said unexpectedly, with a jerk of his head, and let Mrs. Priddy slip out from under his arm and go to Kenny, who was so proud and excited that he had thrown his sign halfway across the stage and was jumping up and down. Then Mr. Priddy turned to Mrs. Dankin and Tammy. Both of them were motionless with terror; he took a step toward them, the knife outstretched and his eyes glittering. "I got a bruise on my leg," he said, "the size of a grapefruit." His voice was kind, almost reasonable. "I ought to cut you and this brat of yours wide open."

There was the sound, outside, of feet running down the hall and of Mrs. Mills yelling frantically, "In here! In here!" The next second, two policemen ran in the door. They both had guns.

Mr. Priddy looked around, confused. Mrs. Priddy took his arm.

"Hold it right there, Henry Lee," the first policeman said.

Without anyone noticing, Sally walked quietly around Mr. Priddy and off the stage, through the wailing mob of mothers, past the policemen with their drawn guns, into the empty hall. Then she went to the pay phone to call Jackson to pick her up in the car.

Leah had given her a dime to keep in her pocket so that she could call somebody to get her when the program was over.

While she was on the telephone with Leah, the door to the lunchroom flew open and Mr. Priddy, his hands cuffed behind his back, stumbled out. The policemen were being rough with him, kicking and pushing even though he only looked very sad and bewildered and wasn't fighting them at all.

After she hung up the phone, she went outside. There was a lot going on. Two police cars were there, and an ambulance, and lots of people. Over in the parking lot some cars were pulling out, but there were still knots of gabbling mothers and children in the lights by the school doorway. The ambulance men in white were bringing out people on stretchers. Several mothers had fainted, Frankie Detweiler had had one of those fits of his, and some mother had been trying so hard to get away that she had tripped over something and broken her leg.

Mrs. Mills had just come outside; Sally listened with one ear as she began to tell a policeman her story of what had happened. It was funny: she was saying that Mr. Priddy had shoved her at the door and threatened her with the knife. He had done no such thing.

Everyone was talking very loudly, but their voices seemed far away. Sally took her sign off her neck and put it down on the ground and sat on it, looking out into the dark at the end of the driveway for Jackson's car. It was funny, how ignorant they all were. Tonight they had seen the work of the Lord and understood it not; they had seen a miracle, and yet had not believed.

The Ayatollah of Due East

by Valerie Sayers

T he Rev was dying: melanoma, and since it moved to his lungs they all knew it was going to be fast now. This would be his last Christmas. It was a bad joke on the Brown family that Vickie had died of melanoma too. That was how the Rev knew not to mess around with the interleukin. Hadn't done Vickie the least bit of good and made the end that much more miserable, in the Charleston hospital where he couldn't crawl in the bed and hold her.

"I don't want those tubes they tormented your mama with. I'm dying right here in my own bed. Tubeless."

"Daddy, don't give up like this. We ought to be flying out to John Wayne."

That was Melanie (of all the names two people doomed to die of melanoma could have picked, they'd chosen Melanie for their youngest). Dark-eyed, tan, she was the only brown child of the four Brown offspring, the only one who'd be spared a lifetime having her moles sliced off and biopsied. The other kids had skin the color of curdled cream, and when they went out in the Due East sun their very freckles blushed. If he thought about the way they used to blister, his eyes filled. He'd never once thought to ask Vickie why she didn't put sunscreen on them. Did they even have sunscreen in those days? Everybody in town walked around sunburned. Everybody white.

"Here, for God's sake. Let me open that." Melanie grabbed the bottle of tea from his left hand (they took the right two years ago, after the satellite lesions and the bad news in the lymph nodes). "Hard to believe you have sunk to drinking tea from a bottle. All those—" She was about to say *all those carcinogens.*

A little late for that. He put his breath behind an answer, but what came up instead was the yellow crud, a thick sheet of it he had to hold in his mouth till she handed him the plaid handkerchief. At the moment, he had bronchitis on top of the cancer. A clutch of panic at his throat, but he swallowed it down with the rest of the yellow stuff. Be enough of that at the end, when he really couldn't breathe.

Melanie set the gummed handkerchief down, trying to be delicate, but then plopped herself hard into the porch swing. "Darlin'," he said. "Don't get exercised. If there's one thing we can learn from the Buddhists . . ."

She swung away from him, furious, her brown calves pushing into the narrow slice of light at the edge of the porch. In the yard the sun teased the pine needles, a clump of three trees he planted in '60, '61, '62. Hopeful years, years when his kids played in the yard right through the midday sun. Now he had to extract promises: no beach for the grandchildren till the evening, sunscreen even if they were just walking to the mailbox. Every one of the six had inherited the curdled-cream skin, even Melanie's. His body was dying of his whiteness, his skin run amok, on fire and consuming him the way Vickie's had consumed her. A fine joke.

"Black people get it too," Melanie hissed from the swing. She'd always been a witch, a mind reader, his youngest child, his favorite, the one who took liberties none of the others would have considered. "They get it on the palms of their hands and the soles of their feet and the backs of their eyeballs."

This time he swallowed bile: that eyeball business really got to him. He had never got over his childhood terror of blindness. Sight was the one sensory pleasure he truly could not imagine giving back to God. Sight was why he and Vickie came to Due East in the first place, the sight of the shimmering marshes, the sun playing on every clump of moss, the look of a place that would succor them. He started a prayer—"Brother Sun"—but got no farther. Francis had never been one of his favorites (he was still redneck enough to resist a Catholic saint). The way Francis embraced his blindness was almost perverse: if God granted you the gift of suffering, surely you could be a good sport and *suffer*. To hell with the sun. It was killing him.

So THIS IS A dying story, but it's a Christmas story too, which means that somewhere in there with all the coughing and the talk of cures and the regretful flashbacks there's bound to be some small bundle of hope swaddled up—some epiphany, you might say. Meanwhile, though, we'll have to work through the dying scenes, the opposite of nativity scenes. And the dying business means the family stuff, because if people get crazy at Christmas, they get real crazy when their father's dying.

"He believes he laid it on himself," SarahBeth said. "Which is so beautiful I don't know whether to weep or rejoice."

Melanie snorted, but Duff put up a hand to silence her. They were in the kitchen, the only spot they could use now to talk about the Rev, and only if he fell asleep for those few daylight minutes he could lie quiet. SarahBeth was talking about the way the Rev prayed to the Lord to please pass Vickie's suffering onto him. Well, the Lord had passed it all right.

"We'd better be careful how we parse our prayers."

"I'll thank you not to be blasphemous, Melanie," Duff said.

"Who are you? The Ayatollah of Due East? The Taliban?"

"Mel. Please don't let Daddy hear you talking about Muslims like that." SarahBeth's lips, the color of modeling clay, quivered. Her skin had a greenish tone too. Melanie was fond of her, but growing up with her had been like growing up with her namesake, Beth of *Little Women*, a saint you expected to expire before she reached her womanhood. Yet here she was, SarahBeth in her green womanhood, and here was Duff in his hateful manhood. And it was their father dying: the proper order after all. Melanie felt she could wring Duff's neck.

Duff was having pretty much the same fantasy about his little sister. As for his other little sister, SarahBeth, he saw a good mother to her four children, one who'd had the sense to leave the little ones at home even if it meant Christmas apart. Melanie, of course, had to bring her two boys with her. Just now they were tormenting their beagle bitch, Nelly, while they watched some cartoon dog on the television. Melanie would probably keep them here till the bitter end so they could see death up close and personal, TV-style. He had nothing but contempt for her selfishness.

"They're going to knock over the tree, they keep up that roughhousing." He inclined his head in the direction of the front room, and no sooner had he spoken than they heard the muffled sound of tree limbs hitting the carpet and the tinkle of glass balls shattering, followed by Nelly's frenzied baying, followed in turn by the Rev's hacking.

"It's a judgment on us," SarahBeth said. "For putting up that tree while he lies dying."

"SarahBeth, where do you get that shit? *A judgment on us.* That's not how he talked, not ever. Jesus."

"Language! There will be none of that language in this house."

"Christ, Duff, you'd think you were Mama." It was true: Vickie's favorite admonition was *language,* and on Evelyn's mouth she'd actually used a bar of laundry soap. Or so Melanie was told—but that kind of story could be apocryphal, something they used to keep the baby of the family in line. "What time's Evelyn pulling in, anyway?"

Duff gaped at her in disbelief. "Could you maybe give me a hand righting the tree your sons have knocked over before they burn the house down? SarahBeth, do you hear your father choking?" He drew himself up to full height, which wasn't more than five-eight, tops, and pointed a biblical finger down the domestic path he thought his sisters should follow.

THE REV LAY QUIET on his bed, picturing Duff's Kitchen Prophet Act. If there was to be a judgment on anybody, it should be on him for imagining the boy had any business following him as a preacher. Duff had no natural feel for the ministry and no proper schooling. The Rev himself had known when he was ten years old, in Six Mile, Tennessee, that he wanted to preach the word. He used to walk up a piney mountain path, lift his face to the sun, and practice at the top of his lungs, lifted so high by his own oratory that he thought he might be assumed into heaven on the spot. He quoted scripture—"I will spue thee out of my mouth"—and he called down Satan.

He was the Rev even then, on account of his impromptu preaching, and the brightest boy in Six Mile High. He won a full scholarship to Emory, where he got a good dose of serious learning to balance his feel for rhetoric. (Duff, he dared say, had never read a book all the way through except for the Bible, and it wasn't too clear he'd read the Bible all that well. Certainly he had sped through any of the gospel verses that might have challenged his rigidity.) The Rev, though, had been lit on fire by books. In college he became a Kierkegaard man and believed he could make a leap higher than the ones he'd made in Six Mile.

When the Rev was ordained, Vickie dropped out of Agnes Scott and followed him to the South Carolina low country, where he'd been offered the tiny Bethel charge. It was 1959. In seminary, he'd become vaguely interested in civil rights. He'd rarely seen colored people, growing up in Six Mile. In Atlanta what he saw disturbed him: the buses, the whites-only counter, the meekness. The meekness disturbed him more than anything, not so much on the women who wouldn't be pushed, but on the men who doffed their hats and hung their heads. Maybe it was perverted for a young man studying for the Methodist ministry to be bothered by that. *Blessed are the meek for they shall inherit the Woolworth's counter.*

In Bethel, which was backwoods but not nearly as isolated as Six Mile, he saw Negroes and whites cheek by jowl, talking, joking. A white woman might rake side by side with her colored yardboy. It occurred to him that he should get to know one of his colored compatriots, but it was out of the question to invite someone local over to the house. He drove thirty-five miles to Due East to talk to the Methodist pastor there, a man with a reputation for forward thinking, who said: "You ought to meet Fred Washington."

Washington was the pastor at First Due East A.M.E. The first time the Rev stepped into his cluttered office in the old white clapboard house, he saw a Harvard diploma on the wall and felt a complicated shiver of shame and intimidation. The house smelled of pine cleaner and made him homesick, for some reason. His own folks hadn't even finished high school. Washington loaded him down with books: Arendt, Bonhoeffer, DuBois. The Rev returned a month later with *Fear and Trembling,* but it turned out that Washington already knew it well. Of course. He flushed purple that he'd thought a Harvard man might not have read Kierkegaard. Six months later, he would cringe again, offering a Nat King Cole album in exchange for Ella Fitzgerald. It would have been more honest to tell Fred Washington he missed bluegrass.

But Fred Washington seemed to forgive him his self-consciousness, his white guilt, maybe even his envy. At the end of a melancholy conversation about Eisenhower and civil rights, Washington invited him to dinner. The Rev sucked in his breath, accepted. Vickie was nauseous the whole morning they were to make the drive and he thought she didn't have the nerve to go through with it. (The nausea turned out to be Evelyn, growing in her womb. Judge not: that was a lesson that came home when word got back to Bethel somehow and the parish voted to oust him. A closer vote than he expected, but still he lost it, and a letter warning against the mingling of the races and signed "The White Knights" appeared in their mailbox as they packed to leave town.)

Neither one of them wanted to turn tail and go back to Six Mile: too painful, after he'd passed his father by. Atlanta was too expensive. They liked the low country, the big oaks, the pecan trees, the egrets. Vickie had her heart set on Due East, the picture-book town with the *Gone with the Wind* houses. Nights, falling asleep, he rehearsed how he and Fred Washington might lead the charge, right here in this little corner of the first state to secede from the Union.

"Think he's gay?" Evelyn finally arrived near midnight, and now at two o'clock in the morning she and Melanie stood smoking in the little pine grove. Evelyn had tried to light up in the kitchen, but Duff swooped down, an avenging angel, to drive them out of the house. Melanie saw his point about the smoke — deep into the night their father was racked — but she would not forgive him for pouring Evelyn's bottle of scotch down the sink.

"He's just a lousy fundamentalist. Not to mention a control freak."

"I must say, we all craved a more *regular* religion." Evelyn was single: she lived in Manhattan and made buckets of money and had not stepped foot in Due East for almost a decade. "Not that I crave one now."

"What makes you think Duff's gay?"

"Geez, Mel, he's forty-one. Does he even date?"

Melanie shrugged. "Who would date him?"

"Is he really taking over the church?"

"He's taken over, evidently. Wait'll you see the fellowship letter. He runs a chastity workshop for teenagers."

"See what I mean? I bet he is gay. I bet he got his ideas from the Catholic priests."

They giggled together, smoke pouring from their noses. Melanie was thinking that Evelyn, nearly twenty years her senior, could have passed as the younger sister. "Did you get more done to your face?"

"Just here." Evelyn wrinkled her brow, only it didn't wrinkle.

"You're doing Botox!"

"Every three months," Evelyn said. "I'm not dead yet."

"Aren't you scared?"

"What I'm scared of," Evelyn said, "is looking old."

"There's a little sign on the front door now—this is really scary—that says MODEST DRESS FOR WOMEN REQUIRED. I told him he's getting like the Taliban. I told him he's the Ayatollah of Due East."

"Daddy doesn't know, does he?"

"Oh, it would kill Daddy."

They both heard what she'd said and ground out their cigarettes, the chill night air clinging to their wrists and ankles. From the house came the sound of their father's coughing. No one had strung window lights this year: not so much as a wreath on the door.

"How long, you think?"

"They say they could buy him two years, maybe as long as five, if he'd try the vaccines. Otherwise . . ."

"Maybe he wants to die sooner on account of what Duff's done to C.P." C.P. was the church: Christ Possible.

Melanie, trembling now, was silent. She'd be damned if she'd start weeping the way Evelyn wanted her to.

THE REV COULD HEAR them—his room faced front, and he had the window cranked open (otherwise, he dreamed of suffocating). He could hear everything now, he found: the wind sough-

ing through the pines, the sun peeling color off the grass. His terror alternated with a queer clean calm.

Of course he knew what Duff was doing with the church, but it
was Duff's church now and God knew he had little enough to con-
sole him, forty-one years old and living with his dying father on no
other means of support. After Thanksgiving, Duff went out and
bought three new pairs of Dockers, so maybe the fundamentalist
thing would be a living for him, anyway.

He himself had never wanted a living out of it: he thought he'd
be freer to shape the church his own way if he weren't standing
over collection baskets. After Bethel he quit Methodism — maybe
that was a childish response, but it was the only response that occurred to him at first. Once he and Vickie decided on Due East, a
plan shaped itself whole. He hunted down a night manager's job:
four P.M. to midnight at the Starlight Lanes, brand-new and the
first bowling alley in town. What better use for a divinity degree?
He was the shepherd of the Starlight Lanes, made sure no one
drank too much beer to get home. His nights were orderly, measured, and he was up at dawn to hammer together the new church,
board by board.

It was three years before he hung the front door, and a good
thing too: it took him that long to conjure the spiritual shape of it.
He didn't want to found a new religion — he was no Mormon, no
Shaker — and he wasn't looking for something that would live on
after he passed. He only wanted a little square house of worship, a
simple dwelling for a few souls to gather and pray for the integration

of Due East, South Carolina. He didn't imagine that his own church would be integrated: he wasn't that arrogant. He certainly wasn't that reckless. Those little girls died in Birmingham three weeks after Duff was born. Greensboro had been ugly. Hard to say what people would tolerate in Due East: Fred was careful not to drop by the Rev's house in daylight, but reminded him that Due East had the first black councilman in South Carolina since Reconstruction. He guessed an integrated church was twenty years down the road. Meanwhile, though, the pastors could visit, set an example. He could plant the seeds.

He made a habit of stopping in at the library every Wednesday, when the Sunday *New York Times* arrived, to read up on the movement. The arrogance of their editorials raised his hackles. They thought it couldn't happen in the South unless they, northerners, crammed it down everybody's throat and stood by while they choked. He saw another way. Falling asleep, he pictured his own photo on the front page: WHITE PREACHER TAKES A STAND, AND A TOWN FOLLOWS.

The Church of the Possible Christ, he thought to call it, but Fred Washington pointed out that the name sounded undecided on the divinity question. So it became the church of Christ Possible. Vickie painted the sign out front: A NONDENOMINATIONAL HOUSE OF WORSHIP. Before four and after midnight he handed out flyers in the bowling alley parking lot: plenty of *brotherhood* language, *the fellowship of man.* The language of possibility. Miracle of miracles, a little parish of seekers was born. Marines stationed at the air base, town folks who hated hearing about hellfire but missed the press of wooden pew against their shoulders. He was ahead of his time, not so much nondenominational as interdenominational, a little of this and that (nothing Catholic or Jewish: he didn't have that much imagination). But they had a Quaker moment of silence, "Rock of Ages," a fiery Baptist-style sermon. People liked their language rhythmic and he could beat the drum. From time to time he even quoted from the *Christian Science Monitor*. When Fred Washington pressed Alan Watts on him in the late sixties, he read everything Zen he could get his hands on. Now he flushed with shame at the memory, but when Vickie suggested baking koans into homemade fortune cookies, he thought it was a joyful thing to do.

Vickie was a cashier at the Winn Dixie and always said it was the best place in town for proselytizing. Evelyn, when she turned out to be the artist of the family, lettered the flyers and briefly considered being the first white student at Lady's Island High under freedom of choice. She chickened out in the end (there wouldn't be a white child enrolled for eight years, and then it wasn't by choice).

The strange thing was the Church of Christ Possible never got integrated either. He and Fred did trade pulpits twice a year. Once they rented a bus and carted both churches to Savannah to see *Lilies of the Field* (back-of-the-bus jokes going, nun jokes on the ride home). Fred thought it was funny that the Rev couldn't attract a black visitor for more than one visit. "Black folk take one look at you," he said, "and know you can't boogie down."

Maybe it was pride that made him crave black parishioners in the first place. Why would an African American want to leave the churches that dotted the islands, the praise houses, the rocking swelling bursting singing calling and responding houses of sublime worship? Why in God's name would they need a white man, a mountain boy, to tell them the right thing to do?

Once Vickie said, "Maybe we should be worrying more about our *own* salvation," and the Rev was so incensed at her blindness that he stormed from the house and found himself with no place to go but the movies. As it happened, *Lilies of the Field* had finally come to Due East too.

MELANIE'S BOYS WERE named José and Raúl. (She'd been married to a blond Venezuelan of German extraction who'd long since gone back to Caracas. The boys were, if anything, blonder, paler, bluer-eyed than the infidel.) They were five and seven and today, the day before Christmas Eve, they wanted to listen to the Beatles. Sometime before dawn they'd pulled out every old album from the record rack along the living room wall, and by the time SarahBeth was beating breakfast biscuits they'd moved on to the solo albums. SarahBeth played them "All Things Must Pass" and wept along with George Harrison. Their mother, once she'd had her coffee, put on "Imagine."

Not three bars into the song, Duff came tearing out of the bathroom, shaving cream half-swiped, to rip the ancient needle off the ancient record. Melanie stared at him through the entire operation and then tapped her spoon on her coffee cup (a little melodramatically) while her boys stood by. Their mother was at war with her brother and had not hollered at them for two days. They loved her with a purity and a force they had never before experienced.

"Let me guess," she said to Duff, "why you chose to destroy my John Lennon record which is—was—probably worth a small fortune."

"Yes, Mel, why don't you just guess?" The last few days, Duff choked out everything.

"Um, let's see. Could it be . . . no heaven?"

"There is no heaven," José said. He was the seven-year-old. "Most likely when we die that's just the end. Bingo. Presto. Like when your dog or cat dies, if you happen to have a dog or cat, which I do. Nelly. Not that she is going to die." José's teachers wrote "precocious" and "very verbal" on his report cards. They didn't know what to make of his platinum hair and Spanish name.

"There *could* be a heaven." Raúl sounded more wistful than his brother. "We can't say for sure. Since we haven't ever died. Maybe Grandpa could tell us."

"Good night, Melanie, what have you been teaching your children?" Duff sat himself down opposite his nephews and wiped his face with a napkin. "Boys, there most certainly is a heaven and any child of God gets to go."

The boys looked dubious but knew better than to answer back. Melanie said, "All right, Pastor. That's your sermon for today."

"Your mama's joking, boys, but I am dead serious. Would you like to hear more about heaven?"

"*Enough,* Duff."

The boys looked up at their mother and shook their heads *no, no, heavens no,* they didn't want to hear about heaven, not if their beautiful raven-haired mother didn't believe in it. If this was a war, their fierce amazon mother was going to win.

Duff reached over and grabbed Melanie's wrist. "Their *grandfather is dying.*"

"Did you think I didn't notice? Turn my wrist loose."

Duff held tight. Now he looked pretty fierce too. Now it was hard to know where to put your money down. It occurred to José that his uncle might hurt his mother and he cried out: "Turn her loose!"

Duff unclasped Melanie's wrist and gave José a movement of his mouth that might have started out as a smile but had surely turned into a threat.

This time they were not even lowering their voices or pretending that the Rev needed to be protected. The kitchen bled into the dining room, which bled into the living room, and he sat in the easy chair opposite the record rack, where he'd been taking in the Beatles. John Lennon was his favorite. He supposed he should be pained by his children's bitterness, but that would have been false: they never liked each other, Melanie and Duff, and he wasn't about to start pretending that they ever had. All this was an act they had to play out and he heard it dimly, the way he heard the television, hardly able to follow the story line but occasionally distracted by the cadences of the actors. Duff was a mama's boy who fell apart when Vickie died and never recovered. His mother had been the worrier—*What if the Klan comes after us here*—and Duff had absorbed all her fear and none of her invention. Vickie trembled watching Dr. King on television (she had a terrible imagination, thought the neighbors would see the flickering through their windows and report them, the way they'd been reported in Bethel). When the children came home saying they'd been called *nigger lover,* it was hard to say whether she shook with indignation or fear. But she never wavered. Remarkable woman: gave up her own schooling for him, read a book a week, could have discussed Supreme Court rulings with the lawyers in town and instead rang up their wives' tomatoes and cukes at the grocery store and refused to see that as undignified. Her parents (and his, if it came to that) thought integration was against God's plan, but she never looked back. A little prim and proper—it bothered him how long she wore her skirts. She would not tolerate an off-color joke.

She had been as terrified of death as she was of the neighbors, and he couldn't say she faced it as well. His worst fear was that he would fall apart the way she had. She wore her agony as long as her skirts, cried incessantly, lashed out at Duff—her favorite. The Rev saw that as the turning point: when Vickie went to Charleston to die, Duff stopped dating the bleached-blond divorcée, began poring over Scripture, skipped meals. The Rev understood that his son was giving up sex and food, that he was making some bargain for his mother's life. He lost the bargain, but the newfound faith stuck. That was a dozen years ago. Now Duff was a middle-aged bully. He'd perverted the Rev's church, but the way the Rev saw it, the

Church of Christ Possible had petered out long ago. Let Duff run it as a business. Let it do that much good.

As for Melanie, her little boys had more patience than she did. And José, standing up to Duff: "Good for you!" the Rev cried out, but the words were lost in a spasm of coughing, and Nelly barked at his feet in concern. Somehow in all the commotion the little tree, in its unsteady stand, tipped over again. He wished he had the will to screw it in properly, the will and the energy, but he could not rise from his chair. A glass angel fell to the floor, its right wing clipped. Raúl bent to stroke it, as if to apologize, and hooked it back on a low branch.

His daughters cooked supper in silence, no giggles or gossip to distract them or him. They had been listening to *All Things Considered* on the radio but Duff switched if off during an AIDS story without so much as a word of warning. Then he slammed out the back door.

"So sorry to offend you," Melanie called after him. "Should we put on our chadors now?"

"Mel," SarahBeth fretted. "You have to stop all these Muslim jokes. It's almost . . . racist. Right, Daddy?" She stepped across the doorway that opened into the dining room to call to him, but he never answered, never opened his eyes. He'd hardly moved all day from the easy chair, Nelly at his feet. His girls chopped onions and shucked grocery store corn, their movements slow and heavy. Where did corn come from in December? Out back the little boys whooped and hollered.

"What in the good Lord's name are they doing?" Melanie said.

This time he opened his eyes wide enough to see straight through to the kitchen, Evelyn opening the back door to check. "They're just burning stuff and doing a war dance," she said. "They're just being boys."

"They're not allowed to mess with fire," Melanie said, and out she rushed. He could foresee the end of this scene: he knew without one more scrap of information that Duff had started that fire, that he was burning something that belonged to Melanie: a book, a magazine. Having the boys dance around the fire was his own way of proselytizing.

He was mostly right. In came Duff through the back door, in came the little boys, in rushed Melanie jabbering away. "Don't you dare," she said to Duff, and from the way she sputtered it was clear she'd started her sentence more than once.

Evelyn, alarmed: "What did you burn, Duff Brown?"

"*Self* magazine," Melanie said.

"That was my magazine," Evelyn said.

"Was it?" Duff was cool as you please. "I suppose you thought it was okay to have that kind of article around two impressionable boys." The boys hung on his every word.

"What article?"

"I would not say in front of them."

"Alternative forms of sexual pleasure," Melanie said. "The cover was just melting when I got there."

"*Self* magazine," Duff snorted. "When are they going to start one called *Gimme*?"

"You're one to talk." Evelyn slammed her cooking spoon on the counter, removed her apron, flung it down. "You're the one grabbing up other people's things."

SarahBeth said, "It's Christmastime. Can't we just all get along?"

"Rodney King said that too." That was José, watching his aunts and uncle with all the glazed attention he gave his cartoons. "But we didn't get along and now there's a war going on in Afghanistan."

The Rev was alarmed: José was seven years old and somebody —Melanie?—was burdening him with the weight of Afghanistan. How did he even know Rodney King's name? He wasn't alive for that.

Duff did a knee bend to get down to his nephew's height. "Sometimes it is more important to hold the line than it is to get along. Sometimes it is more important to take a stand."

The Rev groaned: a stage groan, to distract them, a shameless false gesture, but underneath his fake cry a real pain stirred. Duff was speaking the words he'd spoken all through their childhoods: *hold the line, take a stand,* words lifted direct from his script. But now the words were a parody blown back at him. He groaned again, and this time heard the sounds push up from past his lungs, past his heart, past the cancer's tuberous reach. This sound came from the empty core of him.

A picture appeared to him—a clown, a fool—the picture of the man his children had seen when they saw their father. He was flooded with the same shame, he now saw, they all felt. The girls hid it (some elaborate system of manners their mother taught) but Duff used to squirm and hang his head when he stood by his father. *Those colored men in Atlanta.* Duff's pathetic father. He'd been run out of the real church and couldn't get a proper reform church rolling. He wasn't even colorful: he'd lost the mountain twang, learned how to dress at Emory. He cloaked simple truths in the dead and rotting language of philosophers. He should have stuck to his childhood vision. He should have been a bearded prophet who went up the mountain to meet the Lord. Instead who was he? The studious bowling alley manager who addressed the county council in quiet, measured tones. Wearing a tie. Everything measured: the board for his church, the words for his congregation, the love for his wife. He'd needed passion to make it happen, and he'd had none, and somehow integration happened all around him, without him, and he was left behind: ineffectual, irritated by the weight his wife put on, her clinginess. *So then because thou art lukewarm, and neither cold nor hot, I will spue thee out of my mouth.* Dear God. The words came back to show him his church, a watery stew, Southern Unitarianism. It deserved to be spewed. He deserved to be spewed. He was a buffoon who'd shamed his children, a beached whale with his white skin drying up on the shore, curling up like the devil's tongue in the South Carolina sun.

Once when Duff was thirteen or fourteen, the family went to A.M.E. for the Palm Sunday evening service. Somewhere near the end of the second hour, Duff slipped out. The Rev, furious at the disrespect, made a little show of bowing his own respect as he left the pew, Fred nodding in return from the pulpit. He tore outside to shake the living daylights out of Duff. They'd never been close, never known that father-son toss-the-football ease. Duff had never been much interested in studies or church. The girls all read the newspaper cover to cover but Duff never seemed aware that there was a world outside his family: four females to torment him. The Rev sometimes sensed that Duff found him womanish too, on account of the books. Recently the boy had been stewing because his father wouldn't let him buy a trampoline he'd had his eye on.

He found him round the corner, smoking a cigarette—what he'd expected—insolent and blank. "You put that out and get your sorry self back in that church," he said, hearing Fred's voice in his own. He was aware of betraying much more feeling than he usually did around the boy.

"Sick of it," Duff said. "Bad enough we spend all that time at C.P. It's not even a real church."

"This is a fine time to express your feelings. We'll talk about it later. Right now you march right back in this real church before we offend every single one of our black friends."

"Looks like you care more about your *black friends* than you do your own family," Duff said, and the Rev could recall almost precisely the wave of revulsion he felt toward his own son. "Anyway, they aren't your friends. You just pretend they are so you don't have to look close at anybody looks like you."

A third groan. By now his children had gathered round, the girls clucking, Duff leaning in. Should they call an ambulance? Did he want the Darvocet? Oxygen? Was it time to start thinking about morphine?

"Morphine," Melanie said. "No, c'mon, Duff, he hasn't even said no to John Wayne, have you, Daddy, you haven't even ruled that out."

They both knew he had, but God bless her for her crazy hope. Hopeless hope. Better her boys should see that—hell, better they should see Duff's backyard bonfire—than witness their lukewarm grandfather. He'd played "Imagine" for the youth group once, to spark discussion. "What do you think, kids? Can you imagine there's no heaven?" By then, he couldn't imagine one himself. Heaven wasn't there for him when Vickie died and it wasn't here for him now. No vision of heavenly peace to sustain him, no vision at all, no Vickie, only this groan pushing up from the empty space inside him. He would turn to dust like Nelly. Bingo. Presto.

He pitied them their own terror, but he couldn't face their stares: not Evelyn's blank forehead, not SarahBeth's tears. A soundless wave moved through him and up came a bucket of yellow liquid from his gut. Raúl was so shocked at the sight of a grown man puking onto the carpet that he gave a little jump and clasped his hands in wonder, before it occurred to him to put one small paw to his grandfather's shoulder. But they all pushed the little boy aside as they rushed at the Rev with paper towels and boxes of useless Kleenex and bowls for more vomiting.

"It probably is time for the morphine, Melanie," José told his mother, and sounded for all the world like his missing-in-action father. Or maybe he sounded like Duff: sure of himself, incapable of considering any alternative theories. "I don't think Granddaddy's flying out to California."

A little old man: what had they wrought?

IF YOU HAVE BEEN counting up the fires and near fires, there were the two Christmas tree overturns and the fire in the backyard. You have probably figured out, in any case, that there is another fire to come, and here it is, a fire in the night, which is when momentous things happen.

It was the tree again, and naturally Nelly was involved. But there would have been no fire if Evelyn had not left her cigarette burning in the ashtray, and she would not have been smoking in the house at three o'clock in the morning if she had not been so furious with Duff for burning her *Self* magazine. The truth was, Evelyn of the wrinkle-free face had not slept through the night once in the last thirty-three years, and it was her habit to lie reading and smoking till she calmed herself into a quiet that resembled sleep off and on.

Tonight, though—what with the spoiled dinner and her father's three rounds of vomiting—she'd lighted a half-pack of cigarettes and left a couple of them burning as she drifted in and out. There was nothing to read in this house: nothing but shelves full of Niebuhr and Gandhi and the spiritual touchy-feely fads her father had followed on down through the years. Lately it was Thich Nhat Hanh. She found it all sweet but—not terribly involving. And painfully naïve.

Here she was, though, sound asleep for once after dipping into *Touching Peace* while she lay on the couch, her own lungs perversely cancer-free. She snored lustily. When Nelly toppled the tree this time, all of the glass balls were already broken, so there were only the tiniest *pings* and *plings* that the Rev heard way back in the rear bedroom. He knew what it was right away, but he did not have the energy to rise and right the tree. He did not know, either, that the last little *pling* was the metal ashtray toppling, or that the butts, two of them still alive, were falling onto the moss-green carpet.

A slow burn at first, but by the time the first small flames had wakened Evelyn the smell of plastic carpet melting had wakened Duff too. Nelly went first to fetch the boys and then the Rev before she circled back to Melanie, the soundest sleeper and the last to rise. Even SarahBeth was already up, watching in slow motion, praising the Lord that her children were not there to witness this latest judgment.

The problem was the flames by now were brisk and blocking the front door. Since the living room bled into the dining room, which bled into the kitchen, they could not reach the back door either. One wing of the little L-shaped house was blocked off. They'd have to leave by a bedroom window, and Evelyn herself, seeing the quick onrush of the flames, herded them into her father's bedroom, the farthest back. The smoke was filling the house and an open window pulled it toward them. Duff slammed the door and screamed at SarahBeth to stuff something in the cracks. She removed her own nightgown and crouched naked to push it under the door.

Melanie, even in the midst of all this crazy excitement, laughed out loud. SarahBeth was so modest a girl, she had never once changed in front of any of them.

Melanie was able to laugh because it was pretty clear that they were all going to get out in time. Duff had slashed the screen with a pen or something he found lying on the night table. The screen he'd heaved into the front yard. The window cranked out, wide enough for all of them, though it was nearly five feet off the ground and they'd all need a boost. The boys and Evelyn had already been hoisted through, and now SarahBeth clambered up on Duff's open palm — though not before grabbing the bedsheet to cover herself. Melanie and Duff had not spoken a single word to one another, but they had choreographed the whole operation together. They intended to lift their father and deliver him into their sisters' waiting arms. Then Melanie would hop up, with Duff's help, and Duff would lift himself.

The Rev was dazed. Later Melanie would say he didn't feel that much heavier than José when they lifted him. SarahBeth and Evelyn were there on the ground to lower and cradle him. Quick as a flash Melanie was through, and with a grunt Duff followed. The family was safe outside in the damp cool December night, the stars unperturbed above them, the blazing house a minor inconvenience, maybe even an entertainment, in the exhilaration of their being so wholly and gloriously alive.

Melanie, however, became aware that Raúl was screaming out a warning and that he'd been screaming it out continuously since they'd lifted him through the window. She'd filtered it out to do what she needed to do, but now without hearing the word she knew what it was: *Nelly, Nelly.* He'd been calling again and again for his dog—*Don't forget Nelly*—but they'd escaped and left Nelly behind and now the flames advanced on the back bedroom.

Her heart melted as the drapes and the carpets and the furniture melted. She took her son in her arms and cradled him (so long since she'd thought of him as a baby). Her father watched them with uncomprehending eyes: glazed, like José's when he watched TV. From inside the bedroom came the beagle's panicked bay. Raúl wriggled free from her arms and tore for the front door. She had to tackle him to the ground to stop him from entering the heart of the fire.

And when she finally turned back to see why no one came to help her, she saw that they were occupied pulling the Rev down from the window. He'd thought to save Nelly himself and had stepped onto the metal hose wrap with the intention of flinging himself back into the bedroom. Evelyn and SarahBeth were each tugging at one of his legs to lower him to the earth. The dog was burning up inside the house. Against the pale shingles their dark figures made a black-and-white comedy: Buster Keaton, Charlie Chaplin.

Duff pushed aside one sister, then the other, pulled his father from the waist and flung him to the ground, an Oedipal moment, which resulted in all three daughters rushing to their father's side, Melanie still clutching Raúl. Their backs were turned when Raúl's and José's cries went up: joyful cries, gleeful cries, though their dog had been tossed from the window and now yelped in pain, her back legs broken from the force of Duff's throw.

The sisters turned from ministering to their father, who from the looks of him was bruised all over. But his eyes were clear now, piercing even, as he scanned the window for a sign of his son. The rest of them still watched the movie—by God, the flames were furious—but the Rev broke again for his foothold on the side of the house and it was all his girls could do to hold him.

Then Duff's mouth appeared in the frame, bellowing: "Get out of the goddamned way!" He dove headfirst. He barely missed Nelly, but he picked himself up and stumbled across the grass, his nose smashed but the rest of him as swaggering as ever. He let out a crazy roar of laughter—they were pretty sure it was laughter—and then he puked, pretty much the way their father had done earlier in the night.

They all ran from the rampaging flames. The Rev swallowed breath after breath. Somehow the smoke had cleaned his lungs, purified them, and he could take in deep swallows of air. The oxygen made him dizzy but he wrapped Raúl and the wounded Nelly in a great bear hug and tried to imitate Duff's laugh.

Evelyn said, "Did you hear what you said, Duff, coming out that window? You were *cussing*."

Duff shook his head, humorless as ever. "Has anybody thought to call 911?"

"Look at you, Duff," the Rev said, "you're black!" And it's true, he was, covered with soot, his pale plump cheeks charred in the firelight.

Duff spat ashes. *"You wish,"* he said, and the Rev nearly stumbled from the force of the blow. For one shining flash in the middle of the fire, he'd thought, since they both went after the dog, that maybe his son lived on the same moral plane of the universe after all.

THE VET WANTED to put Nelly down, but how could they, after that? Raúl stretched himself out on the floor by her pillow, where she lay in her splints. Mostly she was woozy from the doggy downers and mostly they did not get her outside in time. The pillow's stench was nasty.

They were staying in a parishioner's trailer on the beach road: Melanie, the boys, Duff, and the Rev. SarahBeth had returned to her children, Evelyn to Manhattan and her magazines. They had all pretty much slept or sleepwalked through Christmas Eve and Christmas Day and many of the days that followed. Stupefying to wake each morning and think of all they had to do in the fire's aftermath. Melanie begged her father to take the fire as a sign that they should fly out to the cancer center and burn the disease from his body too, but he was more remote after the blaze and sometimes refused even to answer her.

Now it was late January. The bronchitis was pneumonia and the cancer swelled in his lungs. Maybe it was in his brain by now too. He told the doctor and anybody who was listening that he wasn't going to the hospital no matter how bad a turn he took. He was on the oxygen day and night. It wasn't even his own bed he was dying in, just some National Guardsman's trailer—and when the guardsman came back from his call-up, the Rev would be dying without so much as a bed. Somehow this thought calmed him. It was not that the terror had stopped—when it rode in now, it was a harder, faster wave that submerged him—but that he could sustain the peaceful floating stretches longer. He woke from dreams hollering the names of childhood friends from Six Mile and it was so satisfying that he took to crying out even when he wasn't asleep. "Why was it out of the question?" he said once. Maybe he didn't sound like a prophet anymore, but the force felt good. It would be soon now. He was almost ready to vacate his skin, and meantime he embraced his suffering with a new fervor.

As for Duff, he had stopped speaking to Melanie entirely, but tried to educate her sons whenever she went off to the store. Sometimes he went and put a hand on his father's forehead. He wasn't sure what that accomplished, but it was what his mother had always done, and the Rev seemed to settle under his touch like a sheet being smoothed. The Rev liked it so much, in fact, that he began calling out every few hours through the day. "I was lukewarm," he hollered from the bedroom, and Duff rushed in to lay on his hands. Skin on skin, flesh of his flesh. At those moments the Rev liked to imagine that they were leaping together, father and son on the trampoline he'd never let Duff buy. That was the painkillers, of course, but maybe even without the pills he'd have this sensation of ascending to a higher place.

Duff's steps were livelier too. The fire had given him new ideas for the fellowship: study groups, the women's auxiliary. He had his eye on a redheaded widow, a woman with his mother's plump cheeks, and after his father died he might be able to think about courting her properly. He was not ashamed that his thoughts had turned randy: what with the mess and smell and bodily fluids around the trailer, all kinds of body thoughts just kept assaulting him. He found they troubled him less with his father dying. All kinds of thoughts seemed possible now.

Snow

by Robert Olen Butler

I wonder how long he watched me sleeping. I still wonder that. He sat and he did not wake me to ask about his carry-out order. Did he watch my eyes move as I dreamed? When I finally knew he was there and I turned to look at him, I could not make out his whole face at once. His head was turned a little to the side. His beard was neatly trimmed, but the jaw it covered was long and its curve was like a sampan sail and it held my eyes the way a sail always did when I saw one on the sea. Then I raised my eyes and looked at his nose. I am Vietnamese, you know, and we have a different sense of these proportions. Our noses are small and his was long and it also curved, gently, a reminder of his jaw, which I looked at again. His beard was dark gray, like he'd crawled out of a charcoal kiln. I make these comparisons to things from my country and village, but it is only to clearly say what this face was like. It is not that he reminded me of home. That was the farthest thing from my mind when I first saw Mr. Cohen. And I must have stared at him in those first moments with a strange look because when his face turned full to me and I could finally lift my gaze to his eyes, his eyebrows made a little jump like he was asking me, What is it? What's wrong?

I was at this same table before the big window at the front of the restaurant. The Plantation Hunan does not look like a restaurant, though. No one would give it a name like that unless it really was an old plantation house. It's very large and full of antiques. It's quiet right now. Not even five, and I can hear the big clock—I had never seen one till I came here. No one in Vietnam has a clock as tall as a man. Time isn't as important as that in Vietnam. But the clock here is very tall and they call it Grandfather, which I like, and Grandfather is ticking very slowly right now, and he wants me to fall asleep again. But I won't.

This plantation house must feel like a refugee. It is full of foreign smells, ginger and Chinese pepper and fried shells for wonton, and there's a motel on one side and a gas station on the other, not like the life the house once knew, though there are very large oak trees surrounding it, trees that must have been here when this was still a plantation. The house sits on a busy street and the Chinese family who owns it changed it from Plantation Seafood into a place that could hire a Vietnamese woman like me to be a waitress. They are very kind, this family, though we know we are different from each other. They are Chinese and I am Vietnamese and they are very kind, but we are both here in Louisiana and they go somewhere with the other Chinese in town—there are four restaurants and two laundries and some people, I think, who work as engineers at the oil refinery. They go off to themselves and they don't seem to even notice where they are.

I was sleeping that day he came in here. It was late afternoon of the day before Christmas. Almost Christmas Eve. I am not a Christian. My mother and I are Buddhist. I live with my mother and she is very sad for me because I am thirty-four years old and I am not married. There are other Vietnamese here in Lake Charles, Louisiana, but we are not a community. We are all too sad, perhaps, or too tired. But maybe not. Maybe that's just me saying that. Maybe the others are real Americans already. My mother has two Vietnamese friends, old women like her, and her two friends look at me with the same sadness in their faces because of what they see as my life. They know that once I might have been married, but the fiancé I had in my town in Vietnam went away in the army and though he is still alive in Vietnam, the last I heard, he is driving a cab in Hô Chí Minh City and he is married to someone else. I never really knew him, and I don't feel any loss. It's just that he's the only boy my mother ever speaks of when she gets frightened for me.

I get frightened for me, too, sometimes, but it's not because I have no husband. That Christmas Eve afternoon I woke slowly. The front tables are for cocktails and for waiting for carry-out, so the chairs are large and stuffed so that they are soft. My head was very comfortable against one of the high wings of the chair and I opened my eyes without moving. The rest of me was still sleeping, but my eyes opened and the sky was still blue, though the shreds of cloud were turning pink. It looked like a warm sky. And it was. I felt sweat on my throat and I let my eyes move just a little and the live oak in front of the restaurant was quivering—all its leaves were shaking and you might think that it would look cold doing that, but it was a warm wind, I knew. The air was thick and wet, and cutting through the ginger and pepper smell was the fuzzy smell of mildew.

Perhaps it was from my dream but I remembered my first Christmas Eve in America. I slept and woke just like this, in a Chinese restaurant. I was working there. But it was in a distant place, in St. Louis. And I woke to snow. The first snow I had ever seen. It scared me. Many Vietnamese love to see their first snow, but it frightened me in some very deep way that I could not explain, and even remembering that moment—especially as I woke from sleep at the front of another restaurant—frightened me. So I turned my face sharply from the window in the Plantation Hunan and that's when I saw Mr. Cohen.

I stared at those parts of his face, like I said, and maybe this was a way for me to hide from the snow, maybe the strangeness that he saw in my face had to do with the snow. But when his eyebrows jumped and I did not say anything to explain what was going on inside me, I could see him wondering what to do. I could feel him thinking: Should I ask her what is wrong or should I just ask her for my carry-out? I am not an especially shy person, but I hoped he would choose to ask for the carry-out. I came to myself with a little jolt and I stood up and faced him—he was sitting in one of the stuffed chairs at the next table. "I'm sorry," I said, trying to turn us both from my dreaming. "Do you have an order?"

He hesitated, his eyes holding fast on my face. These were very dark eyes, as dark as the eyes of any Vietnamese, but turned up to me like this, his face seemed so large that I had trouble taking it in. Then he said, "Yes. For Cohen." His voice was deep, like a movie actor who is playing a grandfather, the kind of voice that if he asked what it was that I had been dreaming, I would tell him at once.

But he did not ask anything more. I went off to the kitchen and the order was not ready. I wanted to complain to them. There was no one else in the restaurant, and everyone in the kitchen seemed like they were just hanging around. But I don't make any trouble for anybody. So I just went back out to Mr. Cohen. He rose when he saw me, even though he surely also saw that I had no carry-out with me.

"It's not ready yet," I said. "I'm sorry."

"That's okay," he said, and he smiled at me, his gray beard opening and showing teeth that were very white.

"I wanted to scold them," I said. "You should not have to wait for a long time on Christmas Eve."

"It's okay," he said. "This is not my holiday."

I tilted my head, not understanding. He tilted his own head just like mine, like he wanted to keep looking straight into my eyes. Then he said, "I am Jewish."

I straightened my head again, and I felt a little pleasure at knowing that his straightening his own head was caused by me. I still didn't understand, exactly, and he clearly read that in my face. He said, "A Jew doesn't celebrate Christmas."

"I thought all Americans celebrated Christmas," I said.

"Not all. Not exactly." He did a little shrug with his shoulders, and his eyebrows rose like the shrug, as he tilted his head to the side once more, for just a second. It all seemed to say, What is there to do, it's the way the world is and I know it and it all makes me just a little bit weary. He said, "We all stay home, but we don't all celebrate."

He said no more, but he looked at me and I was surprised to find that I had no words either on my tongue or in my head. It felt a little strange to see this very American man who was not celebrating the holiday. In Vietnam we never miss a holiday and it did not make a difference if we were Buddhist or Cao Đài or Catholic. I thought of this Mr. Cohen sitting in his room tonight alone while all the other Americans celebrated Christmas Eve. But I had nothing to say and he didn't either and he kept looking at me and I glanced down at my hands twisting at my order book and I didn't even remember taking the book out. So I said, "I'll check on your order again," and I turned and went off to the kitchen and I waited there till the order was done, though I stood over next to the door away from the chatter of the cook and the head waiter and the mother of the owner.

Carrying the white paper bag out to the front, I could not help but look inside to see how much food there was. There was enough for two people. So I did not look into Mr. Cohen's eyes as I gave him the food and rang up the order and took his money. I was counting his change into his palm — his hand, too, was very large — and he said, "You're not Chinese, are you?"

I said, "No. I am Vietnamese," but I did not raise my face to him, and he went away.

Two days later, it was even earlier in the day when Mr. Cohen came in. About four-thirty. The grandfather had just chimed the half hour like a man who is really crazy about one subject and talks of it at any chance he gets. I was sitting in my chair at the front once again and my first thought when I saw Mr. Cohen coming through the door was that he would think I am a lazy girl. I started to jump up, but he saw me and he motioned with his hand for me to stay where I was, a single heavy pat in the air, like he'd just laid this large hand of his on the shoulder of an invisible child before him. He said, "I'm early again."

"I am not a lazy girl," I said.

"I know you're not," he said and he sat down in the chair across from me.

"How do you know I'm not?" This question just jumped out of me. I can be a cheeky girl sometimes. My mother says that this was one reason I am not married, that this is why she always talks about the boy I was once going to marry in Vietnam, because he was a shy boy, a weak boy, who would take whatever his wife said and not complain. I myself think this is why he is driving a taxi in Hô Chí Minh City. But as soon as this cheeky thing came out of my mouth to Mr. Cohen, I found that I was afraid. I did not want Mr. Cohen to hate me.

But he was smiling. I could even see his white teeth in this smile. He said, "You're right. I have no proof."

"I am always sitting here when you come in," I said, even as I asked myself, Why are you rubbing on this subject?

I saw still more teeth in his smile, then he said, "And the last time you were even sleeping."

I think at this I must have looked upset, because his smile went away fast. He did not have to help me seem a fool before him. "It's all right," he said. "This is a slow time of day. I have trouble staying awake myself. Even in court."

I looked at him more closely, leaving his face. He seemed very prosperous. He was wearing a suit as gray as his beard and it had thin blue stripes, almost invisible, running through it. "You are a judge?"

"A lawyer," he said.

"You will defend me when the owner fires me for sleeping."

This made Mr. Cohen laugh, but when he stopped, his face was very solemn. He seemed to lean nearer to me, though I was sure he did not move. "You had a bad dream the last time," he said.

How did I know he would finally come to ask about my dream? I had known it from the first time I'd heard his voice. "Yes," I said. "I think I was dreaming about the first Christmas Eve I spent in America. I fell asleep before a window in a restaurant in St. Louis, Missouri. When I woke, there was snow on the ground. It was the first snow I'd ever seen. I went to sleep and there was still only a gray afternoon, a thin little rain, like a mist. I had no idea things could change like that. I woke and everything was covered and I was terrified."

I suddenly sounded to myself like a crazy person. Mr. Cohen would think I was lazy and crazy both. I stopped speaking and I looked out the window. A jogger went by in the street, a man in shorts and a T-shirt, and his body glistened with sweat. I felt beads of sweat on my own forehead like little insects crouching there and I kept my eyes outside, wishing now that Mr. Cohen would go away.

"Why did it terrify you?" he said.

"I don't know," I said, though this wasn't really true. I'd thought about it now and then, and though I'd never spoken them, I could imagine reasons.

Mr. Cohen said, "Snow frightened me, too, when I was a child. I'd seen it all my life, but it still frightened me."

I turned to him and now he was looking out the window.

"Why did it frighten you?" I asked, expecting no answer.

But he turned from the window and looked at me and smiled just a little bit, like he was saying that since he had asked this question of me, I could ask him, too. He answered, "It's rather a long story. Are you sure you want to hear it?"

"Yes," I said. Of course I did.

"It was far away from here," he said. "My first home and my second one. Poland and then England. My father was a professor in Warsaw. It was early in 1939. I was eight years old and my father knew something was going wrong. All the talk about the corridor to the sea was just the beginning. He had ears. He knew. So he sent me and my mother to England. He had good friends there. I left that February and there was snow everywhere and I had my own instincts, even at eight. I cried in the courtyard of our apartment building. I threw myself into the snow there and I would not move. I cried like he was sending us away from him forever. He and my mother said it was only for some months, but I didn't believe it. And I was right. They had to lift me bodily and carry me to the taxi. But the snow was in my clothes and as we pulled away and I scrambled up to look out the back window at my father, the snow was melting against my skin and I began to shake. It was as much from my fear as from the cold. The snow was telling me he would die. And he did. He waved at me in the street and he grew smaller and we turned a corner and that was the last I saw of him."

Maybe it was foolish of me, but I thought not so much of Mr. Cohen losing his father. I had lost a father, too, and I knew that it was something that a child lives through. In Vietnam we believe that our ancestors are always close to us, and I could tell that about Mr. Cohen, that his father was still close to him. But what I thought about was Mr. Cohen going to another place, another country, and living with his mother. I live with my mother, just like that. Even still.

He said, "So the snow was something I was afraid of. Every time it snowed in England I knew that my father was dead. It took a few years for us to learn this from others, but I knew it whenever it snowed."

"You lived with your mother?" I said.

"Yes. In England until after the war and then we came to America. The others from Poland and Hungary and Russia that we traveled with all came in through New York City and stayed there. My mother loved trains and she'd read a book once about New Orleans, and so we stayed on the train and we came to the South. I was glad to be in a place where it almost never snowed."

I was thinking how he was a foreigner, too. Not an American, really. But all the talk about the snow made this little chill behind my thoughts. Maybe I was ready to talk about that. Mr. Cohen had spoken many words to me about his childhood and I didn't want him to think I was a girl who takes things without giving something back. He was looking out the window again, and his lips pinched together so that his mouth disappeared in his beard. He seemed sad to me. So I said, "You know why the snow scared me in St. Louis?"

He turned at once with a little humph sound and a crease on his forehead between his eyes and then a very strong voice saying, "Tell me," and it felt like he was scolding himself inside for not paying attention to me. I am not a vain girl, always thinking that men pay such serious attention to me that they get mad at themselves for ignoring me even for a few moments. This is what it really felt like and it surprised me. If I was a vain girl, it wouldn't have surprised me. He said it again: "Tell me why it scared you."

I said, "I think it's because the snow came so quietly and everything was underneath it, like this white surface was the real earth and everything had died—all the trees and the grass and the streets and the houses—everything had died and was buried. It was all lost. I knew there was snow above me, on the roof, and I was dead, too."

"Your own country was very different," Mr. Cohen said.

It pleased me that he thought just the way I once did. You could tell that he wished there was an easy way to make me feel better, make the dream go away. But I said to him, "This is what I also thought. If I could just go to a warm climate, more like home. So I came down to New Orleans, with my mother, just like you, and then we came over to Lake Charles. And it is something like Vietnam here. The rice fields and the heat and the way storms come in. But it makes no difference. There's no snow to scare me here, but I still sit alone in this chair in the middle of the afternoon and I sleep and I listen to the grandfather over there ticking."

I stopped talking and I felt like I was making no sense at all, so I said, "I should check on your order."

Mr. Cohen's hand came out over the table. "May I ask your name?"

"I'm Miss Giàu," I said.

"Miss Giau?" he asked, and when he did that, he made a different word, since Vietnamese words change with the way your voice sings them.

I laughed. "My name is Giàu, with the voice falling. It means 'wealthy' in Vietnamese. When you say the word like a question, you say something very different. You say I am Miss Pout."

Mr. Cohen laughed and there was something in the laugh that made me shiver just a little, like a nice little thing, like maybe stepping into the shower when you are covered with dust and feeling the water expose you. But in the back of my mind was his carry-out and there was a bad little feeling there, something I wasn't thinking about, but it made me go off now with heavy feet to the kitchen. I got the bag and it was feeling different as I carried it back to the front of the restaurant. I went behind the counter and I put it down and I wished I'd done this a few minutes before, but even with his eyes on me, I looked into the bag. There was one main dish and one portion of soup.

Then Mr. Cohen said, "Is this a giau I see on your face?" And he pronounced the word exactly right, with the curling tone that made it "pout."

I looked up at him and I wanted to smile at how good he said the word, but even wanting to do that made the pout worse. I said, "I was just thinking that your wife must be sick. She is not eating tonight."

He could have laughed at this. But he did not. He laid his hand for a moment on his beard, he smoothed it down. He said, "The second dinner on Christmas Eve was for my son passing through town. My wife died some years ago and I am not remarried."

I am not a hard-hearted girl because I knew that a child gets over the loss of a father and because I also knew that a man gets over the loss of a wife. I am a good girl, but I did not feel sad for Mr. Cohen. I felt very happy. Because he laid his hand on mine and he asked if he could call me. I said yes, and as it turns out, New Year's Eve seems to be a Jewish holiday. The Vietnamese New Year comes at a different time, but people in Vietnam know to celebrate whatever holiday comes along. So tonight Mr. Cohen and I will go to some restaurant that is not Chinese, and all I have to do now is sit here and listen very carefully to Grandfather as he talks to me about time.

The Holiday House

by Julia Ridley Smith

In February, red hearts adorn the door and cupids hover, aiming at passersby. On St. Patrick's Day, leprechauns, their diminutive booted feet poised to jig, stand in attitudes of arrested joy over their pots of gold. A man-sized Easter bunny with a great basket of eggs watches yellow chicks break from their shells. Maypole, the stars and stripes, jack-o'-lanterns, and scarecrow—the holiday house never forgets, never misses an occasion. At Thanksgiving, the pilgrims in tall buckled hats raise their hands in gratitude while an unnaturally large turkey with brilliant tail feathers eyes a cornucopia of harvest plenty.

But Christmas surpasses all other seasons: decorations up the day after Thanksgiving, down after the New Year. Riding up Henry Street, Elizabeth and Fisher can see the glow before they see the house, and sometimes there's even a line of cars to wait behind. They ride quietly, expectantly; they can't remember what it looked like the year before, but there was Santa Claus, they know that. The whole month of December, whenever Mrs. Holt picks Elizabeth up from her afternoon ballet lesson, the children sit in the backseat and beg her to drive by the holiday house.

"Please, Mama. We won't fight the whole way home," Fisher says.

"I won't kick the seat even one time," Elizabeth says.

They know perfectly well she will stop anytime they ask her to.

Mrs. Holt laughs and turns on Henry Street and drives very slowly.

"There it is."

Mrs. Holt stops the car. Her children's faces are stricken with wonder at so much light issuing forth from the strands of bulbs, the halos of the singing angels skimming the rooftop, the beaconing star, and the internal glow of the Christ child himself.

He lies in the manger attended by the Virgin and Joseph; sleepy cattle; opulent, bowing kings; wise men kneeling in the straw. Eight reindeer in luminescent harness pull Santa's sleigh, Rudolph's red nose an exclamation as he leaps off into the night sky. Flames shimmer at a safe distance from the bulging stockings hung above. Nearby, Santa Claus sits in a rocking chair with his hands on his belly, laughing while Mrs. Claus knits him a scarf. They are entertained by a band of Victorian carolers surrounding a lamppost, behind which stands a large Christmas tree heavy with ornaments and gifts.

It seems to Mrs. Holt and Fisher and Elizabeth that Christmas really begins when they see the holiday house. The season of shameless abundance is upon them, and they rejoice.

THE HOLTS' CHRISTMAS tree stands discreetly behind the living room window, only its tiny white lights visible from the street. A wreath of greenery, brightened by a red velvet bow, is the only other exterior allusion to the season.

This year Elizabeth is nine and Fisher is thirteen. A few days before Christmas is the Holts' annual party—a grand cozy party that Mrs. Holt loves to give. Her best friend, Becky Dalton, helps her, and together they make cookies, cakes, and little sandwiches. They make eggnog from scratch and top it off with thick whipped cream and nutmeg. Mrs. Holt even pays a lady to help her clean the house the day before the party, and nobody is to leave anything out of place after that.

All day Mrs. Holt and Becky Dalton cook and set up the tables. Then Becky goes back to her house three doors down to shower and change. Mrs. Holt dresses quickly, spending a little time on her hair and makeup before rushing downstairs to finish the arrangements. Minutes before the first guests arrive she is still adjusting the food on the platters, making sure there are enough towels in the bathroom and coasters on all the tables. Mrs. Holt loves Christmas—her usual restraint gives way to a hidden decadence until New Year's Day, when decadence is packed away again.

Mrs. Holt is an interior decorator and Dr. Holt is a foot doctor, and the people that come to the party are doctors and lawyers and professors and antiques dealers and psychiatrists and housewives. Some of them are retired. There is also a minister, a pair of women who run a restaurant, and a man who owns a little airplane and flies people to the beach in it.

Fisher and Elizabeth love this party. All the guests bring them presents. They also bring their children, dressed in velvet and lace, or in sports jackets and ties. Within five minutes all the children have their shoes off; their hair is uncombed and the younger ones are under the dining room table trying to tickle people's ankles without getting their hands stepped on. As long as they don't go into Elizabeth's room and break her things, she is happy. As long as old people don't kiss him, Fisher is happy.

The house smells of cinnamon and becomes very warm from the fire and all the bodies. Candles flicker on the mantelpieces and in the centers of the tables, and every time one of the children runs into something, somebody puts their hands out and says, "Careful, careful."

The man who flies the little airplane is called Mack. He has a ruddy face and is Dr. Holt's boyhood friend and Fisher's godfather. Mrs. Holt has known him since college, since before she met Dr. Holt. He took Fisher and Elizabeth up in his plane this past summer. Elizabeth loved seeing the earth from above, suddenly so wide and orderly with its patches of farm and forest. Now, whenever she is upset, she thinks that if she were to go up, her house or her school or wherever she is would become so small it would only be a flat unimportant shape and the people only barely discernible specks.

"Uncle Mack, Uncle Mack," they holler when he walks in.

Mrs. Holt kisses his cheek and Dr. Holt shakes his hand. They get him a drink and introduce him to people and tell them where Mack lives and what he does.

Elizabeth waits patiently, refusing to go up to Fisher's room with Carrie and Sarah Dalton to see what the boys are doing. She already knows, anyway; they are drinking the eggnog *with* instead of the eggnog *without* and they are probably all going to be sick. She leans against her daddy's side and lets him twist her hair between his fingers as he talks to Mack. Dr. Holt is a little shy. Parties make him nervous, and he likes the warm, solid anchor of a child under his hand.

"Why don't you get married?" Dr. Holt is saying. "You should settle down."

"Mack's too handsome to get married," says Mrs. Holt. "He'd be selfish to limit himself to one woman."

Mack laughs, "Share the wealth, I always say."

Elizabeth doesn't think Uncle Mack seems her daddy's age, maybe because he doesn't wear a suit or a beard. When she's older, she'll marry Mack, and she'll serve people little sandwiches and drinks when they go up in the airplane.

Finally, when Mack sits down with a plate of food, Elizabeth makes her way to him through the sea of people.

"Hey, Uncle Mack."

He finishes his drink and says, "I was wondering where you'd got to, Lizzie. I have a present for you."

"You do?"

"Mmm-hmm. It's in my car. You want to go out and get it with me?"

"Whenever you want to. Why don't you finish your plate first?" She doesn't want to seem greedy for presents.

"Good idea," he says and pats the sofa. "Sit beside me and tell me about things."

He gives her a ham biscuit off his plate and then a brownie and a strawberry. She smooths her green velvet dress over her knees and tells about how she played a mouse in the *Nutcracker* this year. She had spent a lot of time practicing a pinched rat face in the mirror until she learned, to her great disappointment, that they would all wear masks and nobody would even know which mouse she was.

"You should come see it next time, Uncle Mack. It's pretty good. And I'll get a better part next year."

"Which part do you want?"

"I don't know. Everybody wants to be Clara, the main girl, but I don't," she says. "She gets to wear a party dress for one scene and then the whole rest of it she just runs around in her nightgown looking at everything. She doesn't dance much and she doesn't have to do anything except smile or look surprised."

Mack laughs. "You want more of a challenge?"

"Yeah. And a decent costume."

Somebody is playing the piano now and people are singing tidings of comfort and joy, comfort and joy, oh-oh. Mrs. Holt and Becky keep bringing trays out of the kitchen and carrying the empty ones back. Mrs. Holt says, "I swear next year I'm going to hire somebody to do this so I can just relax."

Elizabeth puts on her new coat with the fur-trimmed hood and the matching blue gloves. It is cold outside, and once the door is closed they still hear the muted noise of the party, but now it sounds as if it is all taking place underneath a pillow. The tree shines through the half-drawn curtains.

Mack's car is down the block, and they walk holding hands. The houses on the street are similar—all of them two stories of brick or wooden siding with painted shutters and at least one large, spreading tree per generous lawn. Electric candles stand like small sentinels in the windows; the neighbors are united in silent agreement that this understated display is the most tasteful acknowledgment of the season.

The air is brisk against her cheeks, and Elizabeth feels proud and excited to have Uncle Mack all to herself—him holding her hand so firmly and talking to her like he loves her and she is the most interesting person ever born—all while they are going to his car to get her a present.

Inside the trunk is a large box wrapped up and tied with a silver bow, a slightly smaller box wrapped the same way, and a basket, its contents covered with a red cloth.

"We should've got Fisher to help, too. That's his in the big box. And the other box is yours, so why don't you take that?"

Elizabeth carries it with both hands. It's not very heavy. She even feels a little disappointed that he has brought everybody else a gift, too, even though he always does.

"How's your airplane?" she asks as they walk back.

"I have two now," Mack says. "It's quite a business. I have a friend who flies whichever one I'm not flying and we take people to the mountains or the beach and they get to drink champagne in the sky."

"Do they get drunk?" Elizabeth asks. She has recently realized that not only do her parents get drunk sometimes, they seem to do it on purpose.

"Sometimes, I guess they do."

"I think Fisher's trying to get drunk," she says.

Mack laughs. "Why do you say that?"

"I saw him getting some eggnog and saying it was for a grown-up and then he went upstairs with it."

"He might not like the taste. It's pretty strong."

"I bet he'll drink it anyway. He doesn't mind it if things taste bad. He thinks grape-flavored cough medicine tastes great and I hate it."

"Are you going to tell on him?"

"No."

"Why not?"

"He didn't do anything to me. Besides, I want to know what it's like and he won't tell me if I tell on him," she says before they open the door and unmuffle the party and go inside.

MACK GIVES THE basket to Mrs. Holt.

"Thank you," she says, without even uncovering the things. It's the same every year—two bottles of wine, cheese, chocolates, and a sausage. "I'm going to hide it in the laundry room so we'll have something left when the party's over."

Elizabeth thinks her mother looks beautiful laughing in her red lipstick, with her hair piled on top of her head, wearing her shimmery silver blouse and flowing long pants. Uncle Mack's face is newly red from the cold trip to the car, but it only makes him more handsome. Elizabeth believes it must be perfect to be grown and always do what you please.

"It's always a great party," Mack says. "I'd never miss it."

"You never were one to miss a free drink," Mrs. Holt says as she pushes open the kitchen door.

Mack puts Fisher's gift under the tree, and then Elizabeth opens hers.

It is a family of plastic mice, dressed in hats and scarves, standing on their hind legs beside a Christmas tree. The father wears glasses and the mother, in an apron, holds a hymnal. There are three children of different sizes, one holding a stocking, one a candy cane, and the littlest clutching a teddy bear. Their mouths are open as if they are singing. An electrical cord comes out of the base like a tail.

"Wow," says Elizabeth. She feels overcome by such an extravagant, impractical gift. "Thank you, Uncle Mack."

"Your mama told me before that you were a mouse in the *Nutcracker* so I thought it'd be fun for you to have something to remember it by. We have to plug it in to get the full effect," he says. So they go upstairs and he sets it on her dresser, plugs it in, and turns off the light. All the mice glow and the tree lights up and when Mack presses a button they sing "Silent Night."

When the song is over, she thanks him again and kisses his cheek. His stubble is bristly against her lips, and he smells of wine and smoke.

"I love it," she says. "I'm going to show Mama. I'm going to show Fisher and everybody."

"You do that. I'm going to get some more food."

She finds her mother smoking a cigarette by the fireplace, talking to a man Elizabeth doesn't like. He always asks her to play something on the piano. He is about two hundred years old and thinks all girls play the piano and do needlepoint.

Elizabeth waits politely for them to finish, rubbing circles in the Oriental rug with her black patent leather shoe. Every Christmas she gets a new velvet dress, shoes, and a coat. Her mother believes in Christmas and Easter clothes.

"Can I show you something, Mama?"

"Have you said 'Merry Christmas' to Mr. Morris?"

"Merry Christmas, Mr. Morris."

"Merry Christmas to you, Elizabeth. Do you know 'It Came upon a Midnight Clear'?"

"No sir," she says, "but I can sing 'Grandma Got Run over by a Reindeer.'"

"What was that?" he says, bending closer, his wrinkled face and sunken upper body descending toward her in little halts and jerks, as if it is being lowered by a crane.

Mrs. Holt shoots her a look. "She doesn't know that one, Mr. Morris. Elizabeth doesn't play the piano. She takes ballet lessons."

"Ballet? Oh, yes. Makes you limber," he said, drifting away.

"Mama, I want to show you my present."

"You shouldn't say something like that to Mr. Morris. It's very rude," Mrs. Holt says. She's smiling though, so Elizabeth knows she's not really mad.

"I'm sorry. Can I show you my present, please?"

"What present?" she says absently, looking off into the dining room to see if the table needs anything.

"What Uncle Mack gave me."

"Uncle Mack is always very good to you, isn't he? You'll have to show me quick. I can't leave the party too long."

But Mrs. Holt is stopped by the next-door neighbor to chat. Then somebody spills wine on the living room rug, and she forgets all about going to see Mack's present. So Elizabeth shows it to Sarah and Carrie and then to Fisher, who runs off to find his own gift. She shows it to all the other children, making a production of gathering them together, turning off the lights, and making the mice sing.

At eleven o'clock, after all the other children have gone home or fallen asleep among the coats on the guest bed, Dr. Holt tells Elizabeth to go to bed.

"Good night, busy Lizzie." He's feeling more relaxed now with all the food and liquor and the reduced pressure to talk.

"Good night, baby," says her mama from the corner of the sofa where she's finally collapsed, ready to enjoy what is left of the party. "Come kiss me."

"Good night," say all the guests who realize she's going to bed.

She goes upstairs, wishing she could stay down and talk to Uncle Mack just a little more. She likes the late party better than the early party—there aren't so many people and they all sit with their shoes off or even lie down on the rug in front of the fireplace. Then somebody tells a story that makes everybody laugh, and somebody else knows one even funnier and wants to tell it.

She plugs in the mice. Then she hears Fisher vomiting in the bathroom, which connects their rooms. Through the door she says, "Are you okay?"

He groans. "I threw up."

"Can I see?"

"No. That's gross."

"Sorry."

"Will you go downstairs and get me a Coke?"

"We're supposed to be in bed."

"Tell Mama you feel sick and you need a Coke to settle your stomach. Please, Elizabeth. I'd do it for you."

"Okay, but you didn't have to drink all that eggnog with the whiskey in it."

"I *know*. Just go get me a Coke."

She puts on her bathrobe and goes downstairs. In the living room Dan Dalton is telling a story about a dog licking himself, and everybody is laughing. Mack is in the dining room talking to Elizabeth's mother, who sits with her legs stretched out, her ankles crossed. She seems very relaxed, and Mack leans down to hear her.

"Excuse me," Elizabeth says, feeling that she has interrupted something.

"I thought you went to bed," her mother says. She has a soft, distracted look on her face.

"I just came down to get a Coke. My stomach hurts."

"I'll fix you one." Mack picks up the ice tongs, drops ice in a glass—*plink, plink.* Elizabeth loves that sound. Mrs. Holt puts her arm around Elizabeth and asks her questions in a low voice until she is sure that Elizabeth will be all right.

"Here you go. I hope you feel better." Mack hands her the glass.

Her mother says, "If you need anything else, I'll be right here," and presses her cool palm and fingers against Elizabeth's forehead to make sure she doesn't have a fever.

Elizabeth wants to say "It's for Fisher. He got sick off the eggnog and threw up. I feel fine. I can stay up all night." But all she says is "Good night."

She can hear people laughing in the living room as she goes upstairs. Everybody is having a good time except her and Fisher.

He has brushed his teeth and is waiting, looking at the mouse family.

"This is weird," he says.

"Here's your Coke."

Fisher drinks half of it and says "*Aah.*"

Elizabeth takes off her bathrobe and hangs it on a hook on the back of her door. She keeps her room neat so she won't lose things like Fisher does.

"Uncle Mack gave me a kit that you can build an airplane with. Dad said I have to wait until he can help me put it together. I guess he thinks I'll mess it up."

"It's your plane."

"That's what I said and he said just wait. So I probably won't get to put it together for a million years."

"Probably."

Elizabeth sits next to him on the bed.

"Does your stomach feel better?"

"Yeah, I guess. But my head hurts."

"Did you drink a lot?"

"Three cups."

"Was it nasty?"

"Not too bad." He goes to set the glass down on the counter in the bathroom. "Are there a lot of people downstairs still?"

"Not many," she squirms under her covers.

"Move over," says Fisher.

"Say please."

"Come on. Move over. It's cold in my room, and I don't want to go to sleep yet."

Elizabeth is very warm in her flannel pajamas under the sheet, a blanket, and a quilt. She lets him get in, and after a commotion of sheet-yanking and turning over, they are still.

"That mouse thing is so gay," Fisher says.

"I like it," she says. "It reminds me of the holiday house."

"Did Mom see it yet?"

"No, she was too busy. I'll show her later."

"She's not going to like it," Fisher says.

"Why not? It's cute."

"She's going to think it's tacky."

Elizabeth can't believe her ears. Tacky is what other people's houses and clothes are. Bad manners are tacky. Talking about money is tacky.

"No, she won't. She always drives us by the holiday house whenever we want to and she never says *it's* tacky."

"But she thinks it is. She just goes there because we like it. Give me some pillow."

"Well, I don't believe you," Elizabeth says.

"Fine. But it's true."

"Shut up, or I'm going to make you get out of here."

"I'd like to see that," Fisher says, but then he's quiet.

When he has almost fallen asleep, she pokes him.

"Do you think the holiday house is tacky?"

"I don't know. I guess. I'm trying to go to sleep."

Elizabeth stares at the lump that is Fisher in her bed. She can feel tears starting in her tight throat.

"I hate you, Fisher. I hate you. Get out, or I'm going to scream my head off and tell everybody you drank whiskey." She kicks him until he scrambles up.

"You're a mean old bitch," Fisher says, rubbing his leg.

"Go to hell."

Her pale angry face in the nightlit room is hateful enough to make Fisher feel momentarily afraid, even if he is the oldest.

• • •

THE NEXT DAY after they go shopping, Fisher asks to see the holiday house and Mrs. Holt gladly turns on Henry Street.

Elizabeth punches his arm.

"What?"

"I thought you didn't want to go there because it's so tacky," she whispers.

"I never said that."

She crosses her arms. Well, they can go there, but she isn't going to look. Not even for a minute. She'll just sit over on her side, behind her mother, and not make a fool of herself.

She stares out her window, then shuts her eyes tight when she realizes she can see the reflection of the sleigh and the tree and the yellow star in the glass.

"Don't you want to see, Elizabeth?"

"No, ma'am."

"Why not?"

"I just don't. I don't care about it."

"Elizabeth," says Mrs. Holt in a sad voice. "What on earth is wrong with you?" She turns around in her seat.

"I hate the holiday house. It's tacky."

"Now, hush. What if the holiday man heard you say that?"

"Who's he?" Elizabeth says, her eyes still closed.

"The man who lives here. Who puts up all the decoration for people to enjoy."

She considers that. She's never thought of an actual person living here and setting up all these things.

"He can't hear me because we're in the car."

"Well, it's not nice for you to say that anyway."

"Wow," Fisher is saying just to tease her, "that must be new since yesterday. It's amazing. It's the best one ever."

"Shut up," she screams and when she flails out her arm to hit him, her eyes open. The lights are strong on her face, and she sees poor, dingy Santa and Rudolph with a chip out of his nose and the giant faded candy canes. Mrs. Claus hasn't made any progress on Santa's scarf. She sees the flat nativity figures, crooked and leaning over the thin plywood manger, devoid of wonder, complacent at finding a sixty-watt baby in their midst.

Mrs. Holt stares out at the spectacle and puts her hand over the back of the seat. Elizabeth closes her fingers around her mother's soft scented skin and squeezes, imagining that she is ascending into the night sky in Mack's plane. It is filled with the smell of his leather jacket and her mother's gentle perfume. As they climb, the cars disappear into the gray strip of a street, and everything below merges into darkness except for the pinpricks of street lamps and the glow of the holiday house, lying against the earth like a fallen star.

Peaceful Was the Night

by Fred Chappell

Rat was the first to speak. As the stars arced toward midnight and the frosty hills around the little farm grew ever more quiet, he had felt the words come into him. It was as if there was a frost in him that the words melted just as the sun would warm the hills at daybreak, turning them from silver to gray-green.

Was he always first? It seemed he might be, so wily and clever he was, but none of them could remember from one Eve to the next. They did not all begin to speak at once and that was usually a mercy, for such a clamor might have brought the farmer or his boy down to the big shed and then they would have to fall silent, the words shut up inside them and burning to get free.

This time there was no danger of that. Cora Kirkman, the farmer's wife, was busy in the house, stashing presents under the tree and setting all in order for Christmas Day. The farmer, Joe Robert, and his son, Jess, were in the barn on the slope above, watching anxiously. Their prized ewe, Marianna, was lambing perilously out of season. They had brought her in to one of the stalls and now sat beside her on their milking stools. A kerosene lantern with lowered wick hung on a hook from one of the joists.

So let it be Rat, then, always first to speak. Yet he was unhappy because he never said what he meant to say. Perhaps he would like to sing "Ring out ye Crystal spheres" or "At last our bliss Full and perfect is," but his opening phrase now was "A cold night it is tonight." He muttered it softly, even slyly, like the ending of an obscene story, but that was only his usual way of speaking and signified nothing. Yet he was disappointed in himself. To wait all year every year, from one Eve to the next, for the power of speech—and then to begin with a banal remark about the weather.

His observation did not overwhelm the assemblage. They regarded him gravely and charitably, as befit the occasion, but he squirmed with embarrassment. Jackson spared him further anxiety by affirming his statement. The horse lifted his noble head and gazed out of the long open shed into the wide midnight. "It is a hard frost," he said. "Come morning Mr. Kirkman will be glad of a warm kitchen."

That was not quite the right note, either. Maude gently chided her longtime companion. "Let us not speak of morning, Jackson," she said. "Daylight will come all too soon and then—"

A murmur of agreement ran through the others. Come the dawn and the words would fade from them like the shadows that disappeared from the shed's eastern corner with the sunlight. The hours of speaking would be all too brief and only the merciful trance of forgetfulness protected them from a full twelvemonth of yearning. But then perhaps they would not yearn for words; perhaps the midnight feast of them sated until the next feast.

Still there lay the most painful dilemma. If one can speak for only a few hours on Christmas Eve, is not one obliged to say something of import? Or if wisdom and philosophy are not upon the moment vouchsafed, shouldn't one climb upon some flight of rhetoric and flourish an apostrophe or two? Perhaps a poem might be in order, if only one could recall some of the stirrings that spring brought within when daisies and buttercups brightened the turf.

When the words returned there was no rush of babble but a hesitant beginning not confined to sound. For when the animals could speak, their silence had a different meaning than when they could not, and they all looked at one another in more meaningful ways. Jackson and Maude, calm and patient as always, took cognizance of all the others, as if making a slow inventory. Rat was under the hay trough, nervously nibbling and glancing about the shed. His usual foe, Sherlock the farm cat, seemed not to notice his presence, lifting his orange paw to groom behind his ear. But Rat knew the cat had noted him and Sherlock knew he knew. The two milk cows, Pearl the Jersey and Daisy the Guernsey, stood stolidly chewing cud and taking care to appear insouciant. This tumescence of words within was almost familiar to them, it was so much like milk coming down twice a day. Six hens had perched on the rafters, purring endearments to one another, while Champion the rooster, alert even in the midnight hour, patrolled the straw-strewn ground below. In the ghostly light of frost and stars his tail flashed darkly. On the long rafter under the south eave two pigeons moaned in gladness and now and then sparrows swooped through the space, chattering what seemed nonsense. Trixie the collie lay with her head on her forepaws, aware of every sound and motion; little escaped Trixie. She could hear the pig Ernestine caroling in her pen some twenty yards down the hill slope and she saw the lantern glow through the lower barn window where Marianna suffered the travail of giving birth.

Rat tried again: "It is like waking up after a long sleep."

Trixie said, "But, Rat, you know nothing of long sleep. Your naps are brief and nervous. Jackson and Maude sleep long and now I sleep longer than I used to, as I grow old. All the others sleep in short spurts, as you do."

"Not Ernestine," said Pigeon One. "In her sty, in the cool mud of August, she will sleep for hours and hours."

"And get the good of it," Pigeon Two said. "See how fat she has become. If I ate and slept as she does, I would drop like a stone when I tried to fly."

"So you would not care to be a pig," said Jackson. "Are you grateful to be what you are?"

"I don't know."

"Yes, you are," said Pigeon One. "Anyone would be grateful to be a pigeon. What is better than to have the freedom of the skies, to coo seductively to a mate, to have food in plenty, and to increase our tribe by admirable number?"

"I don't know," said Two. "I think I might wish—"

At this word all attention turned toward her. *To wish* was a new thought tonight. They never wished except upon the Eve. One can wish only when there are words to describe things that do not exist. Two could not exist except as a pigeon; to wish to be something else was to describe something that did not exist.

She fell silent, abashed by the pressure of the gazes upon her.

"Please continue," Jackson said, but Two had to be coaxed.

"Well—"

"Yes?"

"Sometimes I wish I had a name," said Two.

"A name?" One said, startled.

A sparrow flew by, chirped an opinion: "Name. Nasty burdensome thing, a name." Another perched nearby: "No name means freedom."

Pigeon One concurred: "A name is a sign of slavish servility. You might as well wear a leg tag as be shackled to a name."

"But look at Jackson and Maude and Trixie and Ernestine and Champion," Two said. "The farmer and his wife take care to feed them regularly and to look after their well-being. Once they confer a name upon you, they will cherish you and treat you with kindly consideration. Is this not so?"

"Not necessarily," said the fourth of the six hens. "The farmer's wife has named me Penny, but she treats me no differently than the rest of our sisterhood."

"She calls me Penny too," said the second hen. "And me," said the third. "And me," said the first.

The fourth hen replied stiffly: "But that is a case of mistaken identity."

"I have had a name for a long time," Jackson said, "and I do not think it has eased my lot. Plowing, hauling, grazing—these would be my duties whether I went nameless or bore the name of the most splendid saint."

"If name alleviated one's condition in life, I would be well off," said Trixie, "for I have had three of them. When I was newborn they called me Fluffball. A young girl thought to make a pleasantry when I was older and named me McCollie. When I was traded to Joe Robert Kirkman, he named me Trixie. None of these was better than any of the others."

"But a name does seem to draw us closer," Maude said.

"To whom?" Jackson asked.

"To humankind."

"I will concede certain advantages in the situation, but perhaps we ought to ask ourselves, my dear, if that is such a great good thing."

"Yes it is," said Daisy the Guernsey.

"Oh my yes," said Pearl the Jersey.

"But all of you who make the claim have a vested interest," Rat said. "I should not care for the farmer to give me a name. It is not healthy for us to become too familiar with each other."

Pigeon Two spoke softly, wistfully: "I was only wishing."

"It makes a difference," said the rooster. "Yessiree, an important difference. Now you take me. For good and sufficient reason my name is Champion. All of you applaud my name because you see what I am. But I knew a fellow named Sullivan once and a mighty fine cock he was. He kept his hens in line, yessiree he did. He held at bay the weasel, the snake, the fox, and every sort of marauder. He would fly at them like a hurricane. But then the farmer's wife took an affectionate fancy to him and began to call him Moister Prissy because of a certain style he had developed in striding his patrol. Well, sir, it ruined him, it did indeed. He became finicky about his grain and he started to show favoritism to some few of his hens. He was taking more pride in appearance than in prowess. Then one darkly overcast afternoon a chicken hawk swooped down and, disdaining the fatter, easier prizes, took off this highly conspicuous rooster. If he'd still been named Sullivan it never would have happened. Nosiree, never would have happened."

"That's a trap I could never fall into," said Rat. "A name is a sign of bondage. I demand my freedom. Like our friends, the pigeons, I can forage everywhere. The granary of the earth is open to me. I can range abroad all across the globe without a servile impulse."

Then Maude, in a cool tone: "So may we inquire why you hang about this shed and the barn and Ernestine's sty? If the world is open to you, why are you so reluctant to explore it?"

"My dear," said Jackson, "it may be that Rat vaunts himself too gaudily. Perhaps he is not so adept at living independent of mankind as he supposes. It is not easy to survive without the humans."

"We could never do it," said Pearl the Jersey.

"Oh no, not at all," said Daisy the Guernsey.

"I believe I have it within me to do so," Rat said, but his tone was milder now, a little meekened.

"You speak," said Trixie, "as if there were some shame in being closely attached to human beings. But I know them better than any of you. They have their faults—who does not? But in the main they are a benevolent and beneficial species. Anyone who gets to know them well may learn to think of them as the paragon of animals."

"There is much matter for debate in what you say," said the cat Sherlock. "In fact, there is much to dispute. Are all of us here not perfect in our own ways? Do we not know that we are perfect? I speak of us now as different species and not as separate individuals. Who among us would claim to belong to an inferior species? And yet man admits his imperfections. He is remorseful about them and prays to have them removed. I would not name man Paragon."

"It is man's modesty that causes him to be ashamed," Trixie said, but when the company burst into helpless laughter, she took umbrage and rose and turned about three times before lying down again. That was her way of showing displeasure.

They fell silent for a little space and could hear Ernestine down in her sty as she lifted her snout starward and sang in an impure but affecting contralto:

> "Laetabundus
> Exsultet fidelis chorus:
> Alleluia."

"That is a happy strain," Jackson observed. "Has Ernestine been sampling a wassail bowl?"

Rat said, "From the smell of her slops when I visited earlier, I gathered that Farmer Kirkman emptied into her trough the left-over mash from the homebrew he was cooking."

"Oh my," said Daisy. "I hope that her singing does not distress Marianna."

"Oh my word," said Pearl, "I should say. It is no easy job giving birth, especially out of season."

As if to confirm Rat's hypothesis, Ernestine now broke into a lusty new carol:

> "Bryng us in good ale, and bryng us in good ale!
> For blessed Ladies sake, bryng us in good ale!"

They all tittered, picturing Ernestine down the slope, swilling and singing, making herself merry on a frosty night.

"We giggle," said Sherlock, "but let us consider whether Ernestine does not have a concept superior to ours. All year long we are wordless. Then on the Eve when words are given we only debate. Soon we will dispute. Maybe we will squabble. Is it not a higher exercise of speech to sing songs of praise and gratitude and jubilation? Why do we not follow her excelling example?"

"That is exactly what I tried to do," Rat said, "I had it in mind to say, 'This is the Month, and this the happy morn Wherein the Son of Heav'n's eternal King, Of wedded Maid, and Virgin Mother born, Our great redemption from above did bring.' But I could not say these things. They were reluctant to come from me. So I made some lame comment about the weather. I was half ashamed of myself upon the instant—and yet I also was not. Can you understand my state of mind?"

"Well, sir," said Champion, "I might suggest that you lacked the proper fuel with which to ignite your language. If you had taken a nip or two—nay, I say even a swallow three times—from Ernestine's spiritous aliment, these high-minded phrases would have issued with all address, yessiree. I wouldn't mind a beakerful myself and that's the truth."

"It is not entirely the effects of the mash," Jackson said. "If the heart of our friend were not already full to brimming over, she could not sing so feelingly had she drunk a lake of beer. It is the season, the night, and the hour to carol. It is the only way we who are not human can pray."

"Now what do you mean by that?" Trixie asked. She was suspicious after her earlier rebuff that her friends here would be all night denigrating and insulting the human species. No matter what they said, she would cling still to her friendly optimism.

"Only that it is not given us to pray with words," he replied.

"I think, my dear, that you are correct in what you say," Maude affirmed. "During this time I have all the words I need or desire, yet I feel no impulse to use them in prayer. I might sing, though not as enthusiastically as Ernestine, but I could not pray in the manner of the humans."

"Are you certain that she is praying?" asked Pigeon One.

"It doesn't sound like the most reverent of orisons," said Pigeon Two.

They listened as Ernestine grew boisterous in her choruses:

> "Bryng us in no broun breed, for that is made of bren,
> Nor bryng us in no white breed, for ther-inne is no game—
> And bryng us in good ale."

"My gracious!" said Pearl.

"Gracious mercy!" Daisy said. "Imagine a lamb being born and hearing this noise as the first she hears in the world." She gave a worried glance toward the barn.

Sherlock said, "The barn is too distant. Ernestine's voice will not carry so far."

"We cannot pray with words because we pray with what we are," Jackson explained. "Simply by being ourselves, we express all that we know and feel. We are compact of prayer from muzzle to hindquarters, from beak to tail feathers, from snout to hoof. We need no words."

A sparrow flew in to perch on a rafter and to repeat Jackson's phrase: "Need no, need no, need no." It darted off and was replaced by another that cocked its head and said, "Words, words, words. Words." Then it too flew out into the darkness as if glorying in the nighttime to which it was unaccustomed. This one night of the year it ignored the shelter of the low-hanging branches of evergreens and slid hither and yon under the naked stars in untrammeled joy.

The cat wondered then what was the point of this so-called benison. "If we cannot use words to pray, what good are they? It is like being given the power of sight and then denied the opportunity of looking upon God's creation. For we ordinarily express ourselves to our satisfaction, only we do not pray in formal fashion. This is something we ought to be able to do when the gift of words is with us."

"I don't know that we express ourselves so wonderfully well," Maude said. "Time and again I tell the farmer that I am thirsty or overweary or that some strap or buckle is galling me. Yet he does not understand. I cannot believe he would ignore me purposely, but I can switch my tail, signal with my ears, and shiver my withers a thousand times and he receives no message."

"Oh indeed," Pearl said. "He thinks of the tail as a sort of clumsy and inefficient flyswatter. He has no concept of it as communication."

"How true!" said Daisy. "He even mistakes the purpose of a kick. He will ascribe it to malice rather than desperation or physical shock. Sometime let his spouse grasp his warm privates with an icy hand and see how he reacts. He will kick like a toad in the maw of a blacksnake. If he had a tail he would whip it about her three times from the dreadful thrill of that touch."

"I despair of ever making him understand," Jackson said, "and I am not one who gives in to despair."

"Well, I have no such difficulty, nosiree-bob, none at all," said Champion. "When I bugle reveille, it takes but a short while for the house to rise from slumber, light its lights, and punch up its fires. They comprehend me right enough, yessiree. It is a matter of being assertive, you understand. It is a matter of being accustomed to the use of authority."

"But have they never risen at night and lit up the windows without your summons?" asked Sherlock. "And have they never slept through your reveille and risen late?"

Champion retorted in an offended tone: "Rarely."

"It is not wise to disregard the voice of Champion," said one of the Pennies and the others purled their total agreement.

"I just hate it when they oversleep," Pearl said. "Don't you, Daisy?"

"Oh yes," she said. "That is uncomfortable."

"I have never encountered the least problem," Trixie declared. "I understand their every thought, sometimes even before they recognize it themselves."

"And do they understand you completely?" asked the cat.

"Yes," Trixie said.

"Truly now? Each and every time?"

"Yes."

"Really?"

"Well—"

"Well?"

"Maybe not every time."

Sherlock persisted: "So what you said a moment ago is not the truth?"

"Very close to the truth."

"Close, perhaps, but still a fib?"

"A fib!" The whole assembly, feather and fur and hide, shouted the word in unison. "Hooray, hurrah! A fib, a fib, a fib!"

"Congratulations!" said Rat.

"That's the spirit! Yessiree!" Champion said.

Jackson spoke gravely: "We must all commend you, Trixie, on your swift mastery of language. Your development has sped far ahead of ours. The pigeon managed to describe something that did not exist when she wished for a name. But you actually denied something that did exist, the fact of a misunderstanding. We all take pride in your accomplishment. Your intelligence must far outshine ours or you could not take such a giant step in so brief a space."

But Sherlock suggested a different interpretation. "Perhaps it is Trixie's close relationship to humans that enables her to leap so suddenly to prevarication."

"Perhaps," said Jackson, "but, leaving aside the question of ontogeny, we must consider the range of possibilities she has opened. A fib is but a small beginning. We may all be able to progress to the full-fledged lie. The lie direct first, then the bald-faced lie, the black lie, and maybe even the filthy lie—all these may follow. Perhaps by the time morning arrives, we shall have attained to fiction. Wouldn't it be grand if we could invent parables and fables and long, doleful ballads of miserable love and bloody murder? Wouldn't it be wonderful if one of us could tell a story?"

The sudden glimpse of these delicious vistas struck them all dumb for a space. Their silence was blowzily violated by the unsteady voice of Ernestine:

"Make we myrie bothe more and lasse
For now is the tyme of Christemasse."

Again they all glanced toward the barn, but the lamp glow was undisturbed in the little window.

"I believe I could tell a story," Champion said. "I could make up something about this same Sullivan, the rooster of whom I told you before. Let me see if I cannot." He held himself in such a tense posture, one leg off the ground, that it was easy to know he was concentrating with all his strength. "One day, as Sullivan was patrolling the barnyard, keeping close watch for anything that might betide a danger to his hens, a shadow covered him up. Then it covered the hens as well. And then—then it covered the whole barnyard. Huge this shadow was, and dark—yessiree, huge and dark indeed." He paused, as if to make a dramatic effect.

But the third hen could not bear the suspense. "What was it?" she demanded anxiously. "What could cast a shadow so big and dark?"

"It was— It was—" Champion's voice diminished in volume and dwindled almost to a whisper: "It was a cloud that drifted across the sun."

This time the silence of the animals told their deep disappointment. Jackson dispatched the awkward moment diplomatically: "That is not so bad for a first trial. It must be very hard to make up a story and tell it. Human beings do it so often that it looks simple. But it must be a difficult art for them to master."

"I am not so certain they do master it," Trixie said. "I often visit Mr. Kirkman's home and see the bathroom and kitchen and bedroom, all the rooms. The kitchen is stocked with food; the shelves are filled with cans and jars of tomatoes and corn, oil and beans, bread and fruit—everything to eat. But there is another room where the shelves are stocked with stories. They come already prepared, just like the foodstuffs in jars. They take down these objects called books and stare into them for long periods and then they can tell stories to each other. They don't have to invent stories; stories come to them in containers."

"All right," said Sherlock, "but where do the containers come from? Doesn't somebody invent the stories that go into them?"

Trixie answered in a tone that betrayed her puzzlement. "I suppose I never thought about it much. I may have had a vague feeling that stories were produced by the earth from the earth, like the potatoes and okra and squash in the larders."

"Perhaps there is a Story Tree on one of the farms nearby," Maude said. "Perhaps the stories are plucked from it like apples and stored in these *books*."

"There is no such tree anywhere nearby," said Pigeon One. "We should have seen it as we flew over."

Said Two: "I have seen nothing like that."

A sparrow fluttered to the earth floor and pecked among the straws. "No such tree," he said. "No such."

"I wonder if it might be possible to construct a story if we all worked together," Jackson said. "Maybe stories are made by communal, rather than by individual, effort. Would we like to try? Each of us must contribute something. That would be the first rule."

"What are the other rules?" asked Sherlock.

"I don't know yet. We will learn them as we go along."

"Hardly a proper way to do things, sir," declared Champion. "Not proper procedure, nosiree."

"If we knew how to begin—that would be a great help," Maude said.

"That can be my contribution," Trixie offered. "I know how stories begin. Many times I have heard the farmer's wife tell stories to her little girl, Mitzi. They always begin in exactly the same way. They always begin like this: Once upon a time in a kingdom far away."

"What kind of time is 'once upon'?" demanded Sherlock.

"And what is a kingdom?" asked Rat.

"I don't know about the kind of time," Jackson said, "but a kingdom is a domain under the sway of a single ruler whose will is law and whom all the subjects must obey."

"I will not inquire what a *domain* is," Rat said. "I shall go ahead and begin the story. All of you must catch up with it as you can and offer me aid as I go along. But keep your wits nimble. I shall go at a great rate of speed and tell a story of large proportion."

"Very well," said Jackson. "Let us hear."

"Once upon a time," he said in an unaccustomed loud voice, "in a kingdom far away lived a Rat. He was king of this kingdom and all its subjects were under his sway and obedient to his will. They had to do his bidding because he was king of this kingdom. So he ruled them and they were under his sway. And that is the story of the great King Rat."

Again a silence fell, a bewildered silence this time, and again it was enlivened by the songful Ernestine trolling the ancient verses:

> "Nowel, el, el, el, el, el!
> I thonke it a mayden everdel."

"I fear that I am not able to tell a story," Maude said. "I am too concerned about Marianna. She has been in labor for a long time and must be suffering terribly. I wish there was something we could do for her."

"That, my dear, is a highly honorable wish," Jackson said. "It seems to me that most wishes are selfish. Since we have but little time left in which we can make wishes, why don't we all make a wish in concert for Marianna to deliver safely and without undue pain?"

All the others showed that they assented to this suggestion and again they fell silent for a space. This time Ernestine did not interrupt it and some of them surmised that she had decided to indulge in a light but refreshing doze.

"Very well," Rat said. "But I don't see what was wrong with my story. I took pains to follow the traditional beginning and the concept of a rat as king is not only a novel one but a practical suggestion for better government."

"Well, sir," said Champion, "your narrative lacked interest. I don't mind telling you that right off. It lacked variety of incident; in fact, it lacked any incident at all. And it contained no rooster. That was its most abysmal deficiency."

"And no cows," Daisy said sadly.

"Not one," said Pearl.

"It was not plausible," Sherlock said. "If that kingdom counted any cats as citizens they would not be ruled by this King Rat. There would be revolution upon the instant."

"There are no cats in that kingdom," Rat replied. "It is a utopia."

"Utopias are ruled by great handsome bulls," Pearl said.

"And all the cows are queens," added Daisy.

"Kingdoms are ruled by those who know how to seize authority and to assert it," Champion said. "That means roosters. A common expression like *cock of the walk* does not appear out of thin air. It comes from communal observation and consent. Your rooster is your only natural ruler. I might almost say it is the will of heaven. Yessiree, that's it. The rooster rules by divine right."

All the hens assented to this proposition with evident pride. "How true!" they cried. "Well spoken! Incontrovertible! No doubt about it! Divine right!"

Four sparrows zipped in and fluttered in a circle. "Silly silly silly silly silly," they chanted and then flew away again. Their shapes were satin shuttlecocks against the graying sky.

Jackson said, "It seems only reasonable to me that the most reasonable of creatures should rule a kingdom. To be able to rule requires both nicety and firmness of judgment, nobility of presence, patience and calm self-control, and dignity of bearing. All these qualities are ascertainable emblems of the equine race. If this kingdom is not to be a dark, cruel tyranny, it will be under the command of a horse. I hope that you will concur with my thought, dear Maude."

"Indeed I do," she said. "It is a wise thought. It is profound."

"Oh, who wants to be a king, anyhow?" said Pigeon Two. "Not I."

"Nor I," said One. "To perch all day on a throne and never to fly. No cockroaches to eat. How dreary."

"I know the stories," Trixie said. "I have heard them at Mitzi's bedside many times. The king of this far country is always a human, an old man with three sons of whom the youngest is the cleverest. Man is Paragon and must be king. Your story, Rat, is an abject failure."

"Oh, what do you-all know about it?" Rat squealed. "None of you could even make up a story. Not one. You're all a bunch of— of— of—" He was enraged. The word he wanted was not handy. Maybe it was not within him now.

"Miscreants?" Jackson suggested in a kindly tone.

"Dimwits?" said Maude.

"Ignoramuses?" said Sherlock. He was trying to be helpful.

"I would take it ill, sir, if you were to say cowards," boomed Champion.

"Stupid-heads?" the pigeons suggested.

"Pedants?" murmured Trixie.

"No, no, no!" Rat was beside himself. "You can't even get the word right. You're all a bunch of— of—" At last he found it. "You're all a bunch of goddamned critics!"

This stupendous insult should have exploded an armageddon of enraged clamor, but instead they all fell silent—all except Ernestine, who from her sty loosed a volley of snores tremendous of decibel and epical in extent. This sound seemed to escape the notice of Farmer Kirkman and his boy, Jess. They had just stepped out of the milking room of the barn and latched the door behind them. Mr. Kirkman dug a cigarette package from his plaid woolen jacket, lit a Chesterfield with a kitchen match on his thumbnail, and blew a smoke plume with an attitude of victory. Jess lifted the kerosene lamp, raised the shell, and blew out the flame. He grinned at his father. Then they went down toward the farmhouse together.

The hills around had lost some of their silver tingle and had turned gray green toward the dawning east.

"I believe the lamb is born," Rat said, and these were the last words any of them said for a very long time.

Angels Passing

by Lee Smith

D o we ever get beyond the images of childhood? The way we first hear language, for instance (old women on a porch, talking on and on as it gets dark). Or how Mama smells (loose powder, cigarettes, Chanel No. 5). Or Christmas: my Aunt Bess's quivery soprano on "O Holy Night" in the chilly stone church; the sharp strange smell of grapefruit, shipped from Florida in a wooden crate; the guns of Christmas morning, echoing around and around the ring of frosty mountains; how the air smells right before it snows, and how the sky looks like the underside of a quilt; oranges studded with cloves, in a bowl on the coffee table; blazing fires in the oil drums as we go screaming down Hoot Owl Holler on our sleds ("sleigh-riding," we call it), then get hauled back up the mountain in the back of somebody's truck to do it all over again; my daddy in his dime store wearing a bow tie.

All my images of this holiday season cluster around the dime store, the Methodist church, and my mama's winter kitchen, which was always full of people and food. It seemed like everybody in the whole world dropped by to sit a spell and see what she was up to. And sure enough there was Mama, wearing a pretty apron over a pretty dress (she was the kind of woman who dressed up every day), turning out batch after batch of her famous fudge. She'd already made the fruitcakes of course, and now they sat in the "cold corner," drenched in rum. Fruitcake at Christmas was the law. Carrot cakes, sherry pound cakes, and pecan pies got wrapped in tin foil, then tied up in bows. If the back doorbell rang, it would be a man named George or a man named Arnold, drunk and wanting money, which I got to give them if my mama had her hands in something, which she usually did.

My parents gave lots of presents; Daddy was always worried about giving everybody "enough." Besides their many friends, we were literally surrounded by relatives — they lived on either side of us, and up and down the road from our house in the Levisa River bottom, and all over town. Delivering the gifts took three days, because of course Mama and I had to sit and talk for a while at every house we went to. Daddy used to order oysters at Christmastime especially for Mama, who'd been born and raised on Chincoteague Island. The wooden barrel of oysters came by train, all the way across Virginia. We had them in the shell, fried, in fritters, scalloped. Like the fruitcakes, they were mainly something to put up with, in my opinion. What *I* liked was the ambrosia and the floating island for dessert.

We ate Christmas dinner at the big round table in the dining room at my grandparents' house, with my grandmother presiding blue-haired and ethereal above the snowy linen. I used to drop my napkin on purpose just to lean down and look at the huge dark claws on the pedestal base of the table—cruel, strong, and evil, evil. I'd come up flushed and thrilled.

Christmas was a time for cousins, who'd arrive from southside Virginia with such long names that it'd take their mother forever to call them in out of the snow—"Martha Fletcher Bruce! Anne Vicars Bruce!" And it was a time for visiting the neighbors, the sophisticated Trivetts, who owned the pool where I'd learned to swim, and who might be found eating unimaginable foreign things such as lasagna; the Yates or the Belchers or the Bevins; or my best friend, Martha Sue, who lived right up the road in a brick ranch house, where her mother made the best cream gravy in the world and her father played the guitar.

My relationship with my pretty redheaded first cousins Randy and Melissa was more complicated. I liked them, but mainly I wanted to *be* them—to belt out "I Enjoy Being a Girl" the way Melissa did in the Rotary Talent Show, to be as smart and exemplary as Randy. It was clear that Jesus liked them better than me.

I aspired to sainthood in those days. But I might have settled for a little miracle, or a vision, or at least a sign. I remember one Christmas Eve staring fixedly at Missy, my Pekingese, for hours, because an old granny-woman had told me that God speaks through animals on Christmas Eve. He didn't say a word through Missy. But nevermind: I was all eaten up with holiness anyway, excited by the holly in the church, the candles, the carols, and the Christmas pageant, which we acted out at the altar again and again, wearing our bathrobes, until we were too old to be in it. There were not enough boys in that little church, so I had to be a wise man, while Randy and Melissa and Frances Williams got to be the angels. I wanted to be an angel so bad. But would I ever fit through the eye of the needle? Didn't I have too much stuff?

At school we drew names, and I gave gifts to kids from up in the hollers, saving my allowance to buy them the nicest things—Evening in Paris perfume, Avon dusting powder, a pen-and-pencil set in a clear plastic case. In return I got a hooked pot holder once, and a red plastic barrette, and a terrific slingshot.

On snowy nights around Christmas I used to sit out by myself for hours, hearing the wild dogs bark way up in the mountains, listening hard for the high sweet song of angels. I never heard them either. But finally I'd go in the house when my daddy came home from the dime store.

He never left on Christmas Eve until the store was closed, cash counted and put in the safe, the last lay-away doll picked up—and if somebody couldn't pay, which happened often enough when the mines weren't working, he'd give it away. In those days, in that town, it was a sin to sell on the Sabbath; but from Thanksgiving until Christmas, every Sunday, I got to go downtown to "work" in the dime store, helping Daddy and the "girls" fix things up for the week ahead.

My job was the dolls. I'd helped Daddy choose them back in October, at the annual Ben Franklin Toy Fair in Baltimore. Now I'd dust them and fluff up their dresses and stand them up just so. I particularly liked to raise their arms a bit, so they'd be ready to hug any little girl they got on Christmas morning. I gave them all names and biographies (dire, complicated lives they'd led before they ended up in this Ben Franklin Store in Grundy, Virginia), and made up long, long stories about what would happen to them once they'd left my care. When I learned to write, I wrote these stories down.

Weren't these Christmases idyllic? Wasn't my childhood wonderful? Yes and no. It's like that awful claw beneath the festive table at my grandmother's house. For there were terrible resentments and old unhealed wounds right beneath the surface in that family, as in all families. Somebody was always going off to "take the cure," while others were always referred to as "kindly nervous." In the parlance of today, our family was dysfunctional; is any family *not*?

I would never become an angel, or even a saint. Instead I would grow up wild, marry young, and settle down. We'd have two boys, forming our own dysfunctional family. We'd do the best we could. Then we'd divorce, and I'd feel "kindly nervous" myself. I'd remarry. I'd try like crazy. (We all do, don't we? We try like crazy.)

My new husband and I would form our own blended dysfunctional family. And even now that we've been married for almost twenty years, I realize how hard divorce always is for kids, no matter what those self-help books say. Though the kids are all grown up now, they lost some big bright pieces out of their childhoods, out of their lives.

For I could never give them what I had: my father in a red bow tie standing forever in front of his store; my mother always in the kitchen wearing Fire and Ice lipstick and high heels; the cousins next door and across the street; Jesus right up the road in the little stone Methodist church.

My mother died in 1988, and the church is a parking lot now. My father had a stroke on the last day of his going-out-of-business sale in 1992 and died a few days later. The dime store building, along with their house, will soon be underwater as a part of a massive flood-control project, necessitated by strip mining. I'm fifty-eight, an age that has brought no wisdom. When I was young, I always thought the geezers knew some things I didn't; the sad little secret is, we don't. I don't understand anything anymore, though I'm still in there, still trying like crazy.

We do what we can, we go on forming our own traditions. Just this past Thanksgiving, for instance, we held our eighteenth annual Wild Turkey Classic softball game, for friends of all ages, dogs and relatives.

For Christmas, I'll make sour cream pound cake, fudge, party mix, and roasted pecans. We'll have turkey and oysters. We will not have fruitcake. My husband, Hal, will make his famous sausage stuffing. My stepdaughter Amity will make her famous roasted garlic mashed potatoes. We probably won't go to church. But sometime on Christmas Day—around the tree or at the table—there will come a moment when the conversation spontaneously ceases while we pause, and remember. One of those little silences that sometimes falls upon us all, angels passing.

Contributors

Mary Ward Brown is a native of Alabama and the author of two collections of short stories, *Tongues of Flame* (1986) and *It Wasn't All Dancing* (2001). She received the PEN/Hemingway Award in 1987, the Lillian Smith Award in 1991, and the Harper Lee Award in 2002. She lives on the farm where she grew up, between Marion and Selma, Alabama.

Robert Olen Butler is the winner of the Pulitzer Prize for Fiction in 1993 for *A Good Scent from a Strange Mountain*, a collection of short stories about the legacy of the American experience of war in Vietnam. He is the author of ten novels and two books of short fiction. His short fiction has appeared seven times in *New Stories from the South* and four times in *Best American Short Stories*. He is a professor of creative writing at Florida State University in Tallahassee, and his most recent novel is *Fair Warning*.

Fred Chappell, former poet laureate of North Carolina, was born in Canton, North Carolina, and educated at Duke University. He is book columnist for the *News and Observer*. Among the many literary prizes he has won are the Sir Walter Raleigh Prize in 1973, Yale University's Bollingen Prize in poetry in 1985, the literary award from the National Academy of Arts and Letters in 1968, and Best Foreign Book Award from Academe Française in 1972. He is the author of fourteen books of poetry, two books of short stories, eight novels, and two books of criticism. He lives with his wife, Susan, in Greensboro, North Carolina, where he teaches at the University of North Carolina at Greensboro.

Richard Ford is a native of Jackson, Mississippi. He won the Pulitzer Prize in 1996 for his novel *Independence Day*. The author of five novels and three books of short stories, he also received the 1996 PEN/Faulkner Award for Fiction and the 2001 PEN/Malamud Award for Short Fiction. Ford received his Bachelor of Arts degree from Michigan State University and his Master of Fine Arts degree from the University of California. He resides in New Orleans.

Tim Gautreaux was reared in Morgan City, Louisiana, and received a doctorate in English from the University of South Carolina. He is a writer in residence and professor of English at Southeastern Louisiana University in Hammond and was selected as the 1996 John and Renee Grisham Southern Writer-in-Residence at the University of Mississippi. His stories have appeared in the *Atlantic Monthly*, *Harper's*, *GQ*, *The Best American Short Stories*, *Story*, the *Virginia Quarterly Review*, the *Massachusetts Review*, and *New Stories from the South*. He is the author of three volumes of short fiction, *Same Place, Same Things; Welding with Children*; and *The Next Step in the Dance*. His novel *The Clearing* is published by Knopf (2003).

Barry Hannah was born in Meridian, Mississippi, and grew up in Clinton. He earned a Bachelor of Arts degree from Mississippi College and Master of Arts and Master of Fine Arts degrees in creative writing from the University of Arkansas. Hannah has taught creative writing at numerous colleges and universities and is currently writer in residence at the University of Mississippi. He has been the recipient of the Bellamann Award for Creative Writing, the Arnold Gingrich Award for short fiction, a special award for literature from the American Institute of Arts and Letters, and a Guggenheim Fellowship. He has also served as judge for the Nelson Algren Award and the American Book Award. Hannah's works have been nominated for both the National Book Award (*Geronimo Rex*, 1972) and the Pulitzer Prize (*High Lonesome*, 1996). He is the author of twelve books, the latest of which is *Yonder Stands Your Orphan* (2001).

Charline R. McCord, a resident of Clinton, Mississippi, was born in Hattiesburg and grew up in Laurel, Mississippi, and Jackson, Tennessee. She holds a Bachelor of Arts degree and a Master of Arts degree in English from Mississippi College, where she won the Bellamann Award for Creative Writing and edited the literary magazine. She is completing doctoral work at the University of Southern Mississippi on contemporary southern women writers. McCord is vice president of publishing for an alcohol, tobacco, other drug, and violence prevention organization and a part-time instructor of English. She has published poetry, short fiction, interviews, book reviews, and feature articles. In 2001, she contributed to and coedited *Christmas Stories from Mississippi.*

Tim McLaurin was born and raised in the low country of North Carolina, where he first made a name for himself as a basketball hero. He served in the Marine Corps, spent two years in Tunisia, North Africa, as a Peace Corps volunteer, and was a carpenter, carnival snake handler, journalist, and teacher. He is the author of two memoirs, *The River Less Run* and *Keeper of the Moon,* and five novels, *Cured by Fire, The Last Great Snake Show, Woodrow's Trumpet, Lola,* and *The Acorn Plan.* For his work he received the R. Hunt Parker Award, the Ragan-Rubin Award, the Sir Walter Raleigh Award, and the Mayflower Cup. He was a finalist for the

Southern Book Critics Circle Award, was listed among the *New York Times* 1992 Best Books of the Year, and two of his books have been optioned for a film. McLaurin taught creative writing at Duke University and North Carolina State University and lived in Hillsborough with his wife, Carol, until his death on July 11, 2002.

Valerie Sayers is the author of five novels, the director of the creative writing program at the University of Notre Dame, and a former editor of the *Notre Dame Review*. In 1992, she received a prestigious writing fellowship from the National Endowment for the Arts. Her novels *Who Do You Love* (1991) and *Brain Fever* (1996) were selected as "Notable Books of the Year" by the *New York Times,* and *Brain Fever* was also chosen by the *Chicago Tribune* as one of the "Best Books of the Year" (1997). A book reviewer for the *New York Times Book Review,* the *Washington Post Book World,* and *Commonweal,* Sayers grew up in Beaufort, South Carolina.

Julia Ridley Smith has published fiction in the *Carolina Quarterly, Arts and Letters: Journal of Contemporary Culture,* and *American Literary Review* and has published book and art reviews in the *News and Observer,* the *Spectator, Southern Cultures,* and *Art Papers.* She has been a resident at the Millay Colony for the Arts in Austerlitz, New York, and at the Virginia Center for the Creative Arts in Sweet Briar, Virginia. A graduate of the University of North Carolina at Chapel Hill, where she studied with Doris Betts and Jill McCorkle, she earned a Master of Fine Arts degree in creative writing from Sarah Lawrence College. She is a native of Greensboro, North Carolina, and currently lives in Roxobel, North Carolina, where she is at work on a novel.

Lee Smith is a native of Grundy, Virginia, and the author of three collections of short stories and eleven novels, including *Oral History, Fair and Tender Ladies, The Devil's Dream, The Christmas Letters,* and *Saving Grace.* Her work has won numerous awards, including two O. Henry Awards, two Sir Walter Raleigh Awards, the W. D. Weatherford Award for Appalachian Literature, the Appalachian Writers Award, the 1991 Robert Penn Warren Prize for Fiction, the John Dos Passos Award, a Lyndhurst Foundation Grant, the 1991 PEN/Faulkner Award, the Lila Wallace Reader's Digest Writers' Award, and the coveted Academy Award for Literature presented in New York in 1999 by the American Academy of Arts and Letters. Her work was selected to appear in *New Stories from the South* in 1987, 1991, 1992, and 1996. Smith lives in Hillsborough, North Carolina, and her most recent work, *The Last Girls* (Algonquin, 2002), was a *Good Morning America* Book Club selection.

Donna Tartt was born in Greenwood, Mississippi, and grew up in Grenada. She attended the University of Mississippi and graduated in 1986 from Bennington College, where she began writing her debut novel, *The Secret History,* which met with overwhelming critical and commercial success. In addition to fiction, Tartt writes essays and criticism. Her much anticipated second novel, *The Little Friend,* came out in the fall of 2002.

Judy H. Tucker, a sixth generation Mississippian, is a freelance writer, a playwright, and a book reviewer for *Planet Weekly* in Jackson, Mississippi. She researched and wrote the texts for Wyatt Waters's best-selling books *Another Coat of Paint* and *Painting Home.* Her play *The Brooch* was produced at Late Nite at New Stage Theater in Jackson, Mississippi, and *The*

Visit was workshopped and read at the Alabama Shakespeare Festival. In 2001, she contributed to and coedited *Christmas Stories from Mississippi.*

Wyatt Waters was born in Brookhaven, Mississippi, grew up in Florence, and moved to Clinton in the tenth grade. He holds a Bachelor of Arts degree and a Master of Arts degree in art from Mississippi College, where he won the Bellamann Award for Art and Creative Writing. Waters frequently teaches art classes in the Jackson area and has had solo shows at the Mississippi Museum of Art and the Lauren Rogers Museum of Art in Laurel. He has published two books of his paintings, *Another Coat of Paint* and *Painting Home,* and has illustrated *Christmas Stories from Mississippi* and *A Southern Palette.* He was commissioned to do commemorative posters for Jackson's Jubilee Jam, the Crossroads Film Festival, and Washington, D.C.'s Mississippi on the Mall. His work has been featured in numerous magazines, including *American Artists Special Watercolor Issues, Art and Antiques,* and *Mississippi Magazine.* His gallery is located on Jefferson Street in Olde Towne Clinton, and his Web site is www. wyattwaters.com.

Acknowledgments

MANY HANDS HAVE BEEN at work in the preparation and support of this manuscript. We would like to thank our editor at Algonquin, Kathy Pories, for her astute reading of these works and her enormous assistance in all things related to the compilation of this collection. It has been a real joy to work with her. We also want to thank Shannon Ravenel and Lee Smith for their warm hospitality and generous assistance over a barbecue dinner. We are indebted to Johnny and Judy Malone for their friendship and book counsel and for housing us in their magnificent library of a home. The Malones, as well as Jane Moore and Ronnie and Sue Barnes, provided us a festive evening of book-related fun in Jackson, Tennessee. Chris Gilmer and David Creel, the best friends two girls could ever have, have blessed us with constant encouragement and frequent celebrations. Carolyn Haines, one of the most generous and talented and attractive people we know, has been absolutely invaluable as a friend and advisor, and we are most appreciative for the advice of her agent, Marian Young. John Evans, Thomas Miller, and the staff at Lemuria have rendered us enormous support in all things book related; we consider them family. Carol McLaurin has been gracious and helpful beyond belief during an extremely difficult time, for which we admire and thank her. Barry Hannah and Wyatt and Vicki Waters have been those constantly abiding friends that we cherish deeply, blessings we're sure we don't deserve but are eager to keep. It has been a consummate joy to work with all of them. And finally, we are enormously grateful to each writer represented here, who responded to us with genuine holiday spirit and the absolute best Christmas stories they had to offer—stories that are truly among the finest we've ever read.

Copyright Acknowledgments